THE SAVANTS

PATRICK KENDRICK

SUSPENSE PUBLISHING

THE SAVANTS
By
Patrick Kendrick

PAPERBACK EDITION
* * * * *
PUBLISHED BY:
Suspense Publishing

Patrick Kendrick
COPYRIGHT
2015 Patrick Kendrick

PUBLISHING HISTORY:
Suspense Publishing, Paperback and Digital Copy, September 2015

Cover Design: Shannon Raab
Cover Photographer: iStockphoto.com/Olga Altunina (Face and American Flag)
Cover Photographer: iStockphoto.com/shannonstent (Wave)
Cover Photographer: iStockphoto.com/Igor Zhuravlov (Birds)

ISBN-13: 978-0692516348 (Suspense Publishing)
ISBN-10: 0692516344

DEDICATION

For Cooper and Jackson, you are gifts. Thank you for the lessons you've taught me: that a father's love is without limits, that being different can be destiny, that faith in each other is more important than anything taught, and, of course, for all the adventures we've shared and the many more to come.

~ "Big Fish"

PRAISE FOR PATRICK KENDRICK

"Put Kendrick on your must-read list, and move him near the top of the pile."

—Booklist

" 'The Savants' reminds us that true discovery is found in the things we don't understand. Patrick Kendrick reminds us that heroes are not all packaged the same, and true faith has no bounds. "The Savants" proves that we must believe before we can act and that we can't *judge a book by its cover*. A stunning beginning to a "must read" series."

—J.M. LeDuc, author of "Cursed Blessing"

"Kendrick's first foray into the YA realm tells a story of unusually talented young people tasked with averting the worst catastrophe in the history of the United States. This intriguing blend of near-future science fiction, international political thriller, and apocalyptic tale revolves around the titular group of savants, and these well-developed characters are inspiring and undeniably endearing. The novel is powered by pedal-to-the-metal pacing, a seamless narrative, and subtle symbolism. Indeed, to classify this solely a YA novel does it a great disservice, as it will likely appeal to young and old readers alike. A thriller that many readers may find hard to put down."

—*Kirkus Reviews*

THE SAVANTS

PATRICK KENDRICK

PROLOGUE

February 5, 1958: an Air Force Training Mission off the coast of Georgia.

The B-47 Stratojet Bomber rocked back and forth in the violent air as if it were already ditched in the whitecaps of the Atlantic Ocean. Its olive-green fuselage shone black and slick, like the skin of a breaching whale just over the storm-tossed sea.

A lightning streaked sky lit up the faces of Captain Christopher Blackwell and his co-pilot, Airman First Class David DeRubbio, as they sweated over the controls of the bucking bomber. Rain pummeled the windshield of the craft and leaked through the rivets that held the flimsy glass.

"They could've picked a better night for us to train," said Blackwell, his brow knotted, his eyes glancing at the picture of his wife tucked into the bezel of the altimeter. The instrument read eight hundred feet above sea level. If anything happened at that altitude, they would have had little time to recover, or bail out of the plane, but these were not viable options considering their payload.

"You can say that again, Captain," said DeRubbio, peering through the darkened cabin at the gigantic device secured with canvas straps in the back. It was an enormous gray cylinder with the letters and numbers: "Mk-15-Mod-O" stenciled in white block letters on its side.

"You're not letting a little thing like an armed hydrogen bomb make you nervous, are you, pal?" said Blackwell, trying to lighten the moment.

"They say it's a hundred times stronger than the one they dropped on Hiroshima," replied DeRubbio, swallowing dryly.

"I wouldn't want to find out," Blackwell said. "Where the hell is that wingman, anyway? Supposed to have been up here over a half-hour ago."

An F-86 Saber Jet flew through the sky approximately three hundred feet below the bomber. Its radio was malfunctioning as its pilot, Captain Dennis Cross, tapped on the gauges and repeatedly flipped the toggle on the radio.

"Saber-One to Big Daddy, come in, please. Do you read me?"

The radio answered back with a static hiss.

"Saber-One to Base-One, do you copy?" said Cross, adjusting the gain knob on the radio. He glanced at his fuel gauge. It was below a quarter tank. "Saber-One to Big Daddy, if you can hear me, I'm in the ballpark but do not have a visual on you yet. I'm gonna go above this storm and see if I can see you." He pulled the nose of the jet up and began to ascend.

A broken message came across the bomber's radio. "Base-One to Big Daddy, you guys see Saber-One yet?"

Blackwell nodded to his co-pilot, giving him the okay to do the talking. "That's a negative, sir," said DeRubbio, a drop of icy sweat rolling off his chin.

"We think his radio is out, but he is in your vicinity," came the message from the base station. "Keep an eye out. As soon as you can get a viz, signal with your lights and get 'em to follow you back. We're going to scrub the mission. It's getting too dicey out there."

DeRubbio sighed with relief. "You got that right, Base. As soon as we...wait! What's that, Captain....?"

Captain Blackwell looked at the radar screen just as a tiny green blip appeared from nowhere.

"Damn!" he shouted, trying to remain in control of his emotions as well as the plane. He pulled back quickly on the controls, moving to the right, trying to bank a sharp turn.

The jet continued to ascend even as Cross saw the hulking black silhouette of the bomber above him and tried to turn his craft as well. They almost completed the evasive maneuvers, but the wings of the two aircrafts collided at the last second and splintered into shards, metal wrenched apart emitting the sounds of a screaming banshee. The Saber Jet's wing burst into flame, then ripped away from the fuselage of the jet, falling into the sea like a dropped torch. The jet vanished into the night like a missile gone astray. The bomber continued on, a gaping wound in its wing and one of its engines fully aflame.

"May-day, may-day," DeRubbio yelled into the mike. "We've been hit!"

At the Air Force base tower, a cadre of men in dark blue uniforms and sparkling brass buttons gathered around the control board and began barking orders to anyone who would listen. A cold, electric fear filled every person in the room as they all realized the enormity of this lapse of judgment, this historical miscalculation.

General Randolph Pearsal approached the group of frantic men huddled around the communications console. His face was shaped like a flint arrow head, his hair slicked back, the color of nickel. "What the hell just happened?" he inquired.

The communications officer looked up at the general, his shirt collar ringed with sweat, his lips trembling as he spoke. "We think Saber-One just collided with the bomber..."

"Are they still intact?"

"Saber-One is lost. We don't know for sure about the bomber. Communications are sporadic at best. We believe they are still flying."

General Pearsal's eyes scanned the radar screen, trying to see any image that might resemble a bomber, but saw only blotches. "Are they over land?" he asked, his voice almost a whisper.

"We're not sure, sir," the man at the console said, his Adam's apple like a stone in his throat.

Pearsal turned his heated stare onto the Comm Officer. "Not sure? That bomber is carrying a live hydrogen bomb, officer. Let's try to find out." He grabbed the microphone from the man and barked into it. "Big Daddy, this is General Pearsal. What's your status?"

Following a relentless silence, a scratchy voice came over the radio: "We've lost...engine and might lose the wing. We've got...

leveled…losing altitude fast…coming in hot."

General Pearsal recognized the voice of Captain Blackwell and responded, "The hell you are, Captain. You've got a live payload on that bird. You are not to land. Do you hear me? I repeat, you are not to land with that payload."

There was no reply, then the silence was broken only by crackling static. "What are…supposed to do? We're com…in now!"

The General looked around the room, hoping some smart go-getter would step up and hand him a better decision than the one he had, but none came forth. "Damn it!" he barked. He picked up the mike and gripped it like the handle of a gun. "How far out are you, Big Daddy?"

"…still a couple miles off shore…I think…we…can make it…"

The General's muscles visibly rippled through his jaw as he clenched his teeth and hissed the order. "Listen, Captain and do exactly as I say. I want you to get as close to the water as you can."

More crackling, then, "Okay, General…now what?"

The general's face and neck were shining now, as he said, "I want you to jettison the payload."

There was an interminable silence before the captain came back. "Did you say jettison, sir?"

"You heard me, man," said the general. "If you are still over the water, do it now. If you are not over the water, get back over the ocean. You cannot land hot with that armament. If you can't dump the payload, you're going to have to ditch the plane in the sea. Do you understand? The seas are rough. I don't know when, or if, we can get to you." He paused as if to reflect on his own words. Then, "Those are your orders, Captain. There are no other contingencies. Do you copy?"

There was a sigh of relief heard across the communications room as Captain Blackwell responded, "Yes, sir."

Blackwell looked into the eyes of DeRubbio. The look they shared was filled with regret, doubt, and fear.

The bomber was so close to the water now, that waves were slapping its belly.

Blackwell nodded to DeRubbio and the airman practically leapt from his seat and lunged back toward their deadly load. "Here goes," he said, grabbing a bright red lever. He hesitated for a moment; it was not an easy decision to unleash a nuclear bomb on the world, no matter how bad the circumstances were.

Blackwell felt the ocean tugging at his craft, slowing them. In another moment, they would be in the sea. He began to pull up on his controls, the remaining engines whining their disapproval, as he yelled back to the airman, "Do it! I don't know how much longer I can keep this thing steady."

DeRubbio winced as he pulled the lever and the bomb doors opened. They were so close to the sea, water splashed in and soaked DeRubbio. He gripped a second lever, his wet hands slipping as the plane lurched from one side to the next. The airman fell forward awkwardly and depressed the "away" handle. The bomb dropped as if it weighed more than the Earth itself and plunged into the waves, a white waterspout leaping up and spraying against the closing bomb doors.

Blackwell lurched to the right, dipping the bomber's wing into the water, but he managed to keep the plane aloft. Within seconds, the rain-slicked, black surface of the air base runway appeared. They were coming in too fast, one wing fully aflame now, the controls like the horns of a bucking bull in the captain's hands. Big Daddy slammed into the runway, the front tire bursting like a party balloon, but the landing gear held as the tail end skidded around tearing up asphalt, screeching. Then, it was over. The plane stopped skidding. Smoke began to pour into the cabin. Blackwell and DeRubbio made their way to the side door and bailed from the plane.

The men watched in the distance as headlights raced their way from the base. They looked back at the plane and watched the flames consume the hull of the craft, defying the rain that beat against their faces.

On the ocean floor, the gray hulk dug into the sandy bottom with a dull thud heard only by the startled sea life. It sat for a moment as if considering its whereabouts. Then it began to follow the natural slope of the ocean floor and continued to slide into the silent depths.

CHAPTER ONE

Present time. Location: off the east coast of the United States, near the Cape Hatteras National Seashore. The bottom of the ocean.

The nuclear device that was jettisoned, then lost, over fifty years earlier, the one tagged Mk-15-Mod-O, detonated. The resultant shockwave found one of Earth's blemishes, a fault line that ran roughly parallel to the North Carolina coast, and pushed into it like a giant hand parting clouds. The ocean floor slowly began to tear apart like old canvas. The ocean responded by vomiting up a small but forceful wall of a wave toward the eastern coast of the United States. By the time it hit shore, it was only about a foot high but was over three hundred miles long. The sea water carried inland some ten miles and caused flooding and water damage to homes that would generate billions of dollars' worth of insurance claims. Only one person died; a man who had been working on an electrical problem in his home when it flooded. But, there were some people missing, including the crews of some fishing boats that were close to shore when the wave came in, then withdrew, creating a natural vacuum that tugged the boats out to sea, then tumbled them like toys in a giant bathtub.

***

Three days later: Bar Harbor, Maine. The Bar Harbor Behavioral Research Foundation, nicknamed, "The Beehive," by locals.

It was an enormous, run-down, New England boarding house that had been refurbished into a private, behavioral studies institute some fifteen years earlier. It sat on the side of a mountain overlooking the sea and the craggy shoreline. From up on its mountain perch, lobster fishing boats looked like motorized models in the pristine waters of the Atlantic as waves crashed on the rocks and dripped white, sea foam down their sides like melting ice cream.

Within the institute, Dr. Stephen Pevnick was dressed in his usual attire—that of a typical New England academician: utilitarian shoes that looked more like those worn by a Ukrainian factory worker; un-ironed khaki pants and rumpled tweed jacket, worn by a face that belonged to a man who had dedicated himself to behavioral research. It was a compassionate face, though older in appearance than its actual years, surrounded by curly, salt and pepper hair. He watched with caring eyes as James Tramwell prepared breakfast.

"Exactly twenty-six grams, James?" asked Pevnick.

James nodded, mechanically, as he measured and poured the cereal into a bowl, followed by an equally measured amount of milk. "You know how it has to be with me, doctor," James said, his Liverpool accent so thick it made him difficult to understand. "I should be able to eat my breakfast in twenty-six bites, approximately one gram per bite. But yesterday it took me twenty-seven bites. I may have slipped when adding the milk. That was why I was off a bit yesterday. You know, on my thinking."

"I understand, James," Pevnick said and made another note in a small Steno pad where he kept his observations until he had them transcribed later.

James went through the ritual of counting his clothes before he sat down to his breakfast. He counted his socks, shoes, pants, and shirt, which he kept buttoned up to the very top button. He counted each button. He pulled up the edge of his underwear to include them in the count. The clothes did not match but that was of no consequence to James. He picked up his spoon preparing to eat, but then carefully placed it back down next to the bowl and began to count his clothes again.

James was nineteen years old. His hair was short and appeared to have been cut by dull kitchen shears, which it was. He styled it himself with no conscious thought of what others might think of its appearance. Such things did not matter to him. His hair grew and he cut it to keep it out of his eyes. Grooming habits were necessary because he had to go into the "outside world" and deal with "regular" people.

His glasses were so thick, he looked like he was peering through the bottom of soda bottles. He was a prodigious savant and a mathematical genius, but he had trouble dressing himself. He knew this and, to assure himself, he counted his clothes repeatedly. He, like most savants, had little interaction with other people as he did not possess acceptable social skills. This fact did not bother him either.

"There are eight pieces of clothing, James," Pevnick remarked.

"Are you sure?" said James.

"Are you?"

"Yes. Counting my belt and underwear," he looked at Dr. Pevnick's jacket. "Do you mind if I count your threads? While I eat my breakfast?"

Pevnick smiled benignly. "Not at all, James." He sat down across the table from James who glanced up at him occasionally, squinting at the professor's clothing. At one point he stopped and touched the fabric of Dr. Pevnick's jacket.

"How are the other...*special* students, Dr. Pevnick?"

"Everyone seems fine this morning. It's hard to tell with some, though."

James nodded his understanding. "Do you really think your experiment can work?" he asked.

"I think it's an interesting premise," Dr. Pevnick admitted. "It's never been done before; a group of savants working on a common project. It could give us much more insight into people like yourself. I'm excited about it. What do you think?"

"I think you have too much time on your hands."

Pevnick chuckled.

"One hundred thirty-two, by the way."

"Huh?"

"The jacket. That's a nice piece of cloth with over one hundred thirty threads per inch. In each direction."

Pevnick looked down at his jacket and absently fingered the material. "Yes," he said, and after some pause, "my wife gave it to me."

"I counted them, you know. The threads, I mean."

Pevnick shook his head and smiled again. "James, I'd like to make you lead on the project."

James pondered the statement for a moment. Then, "Because I'm the smartest?"

"That's hard to say. But…"

"I know. I'm the most *functional.*"

"Well, there's no arguing that. You are the only one who has a job, can live on your own, pay bills, do what…"

"What *normal* people do?"

"Yes. But, also with your language abilities, I'm hoping you can link the group, so to speak," said Pevnick. "Etta speaks mostly Japanese, though she is learning English astonishingly quick. Jeremy is French. He speaks more English than I had imagined, but he is *echolalic*; that is, he repeats things, so he's difficult to comprehend most of the time. Harvey speaks English, of course, but he's so *coprolalic*, uh, you know, cussing all the time, that it's difficult to follow his conversations as well."

"Why do we have to speak English, doctor?"

"Well, that's my weakness. My only other language is Latin. No help, there, I'm afraid."

"*Ita is est?*"

Pevnick grinned at the translation. It was Latin, of course. "Yes, *and so it is.*"

"You should learn *my* language."

"Hmm. The 'Manti' you wrote about?"

James nodded and finished his breakfast. After his last bite, he silently mouthed, "Twenty-Six."

"I wish I had the time," Pevnick continued, "but, by your own definition, your language was developed for savants. I've read your book and, frankly, it's way over my head."

James grinned, gloating. "Do you mean to say that I am smarter than you?"

Pevnick shook his head but couldn't help but smile. He jotted down a quick note to himself: *Savants do have egos.* "The symbols you expressed stand for phrases, rather than individual words, and there are so many of them," he said. "I only have the group for one month. I couldn't learn your language in that short amount of time."

"I understand."

"So, will you take the lead?"

James looked down at his feet, trying to remember if he'd counted his shoes while doing his daily ritual. He leaned down to assure the loops of the laces of both shoes were uniform, then looked back to Pevnick's face as if seeing him for the first time. "If it makes you happy, doctor."

Pevnick frowned in wonderment. "It would please me, very much, yes. Thank you. It doesn't have to be all work. I'd like to see how you and the others react to each other as well. Maybe we can drive out to the ocean…"

"The beach?" said James, as if Pevnick had suggested visiting a radioactive dump site.

"Yes. I understand Etta loves the ocean."

"I can't do that," said James, his face stoic.

"Why? It's beautiful this time of the year."

"I'm sure it is. But, I would have to count all the pebbles on the beach. It's really quite distracting. It hurts my head. Sometimes I have seizures from the overload."

"Ah, yes. I'm sorry. I forgot."

"You've spent your life studying persons like myself, Dr. Pevnick. I've read your books. It almost seems as though you admire savants."

"Admire?" The doctor paused to consider the young man's assertion. "Yes. I suppose I do."

"Why, doctor? Why would you admire a group of people who commonly have some sort of brain damage?"

"I don't know. We are all drawn to something in life, I guess. Maybe because you are all so unique…like works of art. Some people don't understand art. Some people love every nuance of it. Yes, James, I do admire you."

James pondered Pevnick's words for a moment, then bluntly asked, "Would you have liked your son to be like me? If he had lived, I mean."

Pevnick tried not to react to the clumsy question. An image flashed into his mind of a truck's headlights jumping into the path of his own car, the sudden horrendous impact of light, broken glass, and crunching metal ripping apart his family and his life. Blood covering him, his wife, and his son. He blinked his eyes, suddenly moist, and gazed out the window for a moment before answering. "I…don't know, James."

"Do you think God took your family?"

"No, James…I know you are very devoted to your faith but…" he paused, trying to find the words.

"But, what?"

"I don't believe in God," said Pevnick, abruptly. Then, he got up, his legs weak beneath him, and left the room.

CHAPTER TWO

James Tramwell: Congenital Savant

England. Fifteen years ago.

In Liverpool, Mrs. Alice Tramwell dressed her "dolly" child in a suit she'd found for him in a consignment shop. James was small and silent—there was something wrong with him, they knew, but she loved him and pampered him as much as her patience would allow. Within a year of his birth, he exhibited signs of "something along the autism spectrum," the doctors said, though an exact diagnosis was not forthcoming.

Whatever the malady was, it was enough for George Tramwell, the father, to become uncomfortable with his son to the point of staying away from home as much as possible. He did this so much he had found another woman, one with *normal* children, and divorced Alice Tramwell so he could marry that *normal* woman and continue a *normal* life.

Dressing James was a challenge. He was constantly trying to rearrange the buttons on his shirts or untie his shoes and, though he could not talk, he seemed to be counting everything within eyesight and placing it into neat piles. This was fine when Alice did her laundry, but became a real challenge when she dressed him for special occasions, such as the one they were attending that day at church. The Tramwells were devout Catholics and went every

Sunday, where Alice would pray to God to help *fix* James while he would sit next to her and stare at the floor. Alice would then stay after the service and talk to Father MacMillan who, eventually, agreed to allow James to go through communion, even though he had not been trained in the practice and had never gone through confession or even a catechism school to prepare him.

MacMillan and Alice agreed that whatever was wrong with James, it almost guaranteed he would not be able to lead a normal life, perhaps not even a very long life, and his young soul would at least be blessed and hold the body of Christ if he were to depart this physical world before too long.

James was used to being fed, though he was now four years old and should be feeding himself. So, communion would be easy. Father MacMillan would hold out a communion wafer and, God willing, little James would open his mouth like a hungry baby bird and swallow it up. The same with the wine.

James sat next to his mother as she stood, sat, kneeled, stood again, sang some songs, prayed some prayers. He felt like an overstuffed sausage (a *banger*, his mother called them) in his tightly buttoned vest and suit coat, his ironed trousers, swinging his small, tied and polished dress shoes and kicking the back of the pew in front of him. He held his hands over his ears because the noise was so loud in the church that it made him dizzy.

When the time came in the ceremony for the communion, a man came and stood by the end of the pew where James and his mother were sitting. He waved them out and James was confused— he thought they were leaving—but his mother pulled him by the hand and began to inch toward the front of the church.

James was frightened. He had never been to the front of the church where the altar, as his mother referred to it, was. That's where the priest stood and did the strange things he did; waving his arms, bowing over golden goblets and ringing small bells from time to time. Where he sometimes spoke in a different language and looked down sternly on the people who came to see him every week, like a rock star, like The Beatles— a musical group that James was fond of listening to. He liked music, all types of music, and listened to old rock music, such as The Beatles and The Rolling Stones and an Irish band called U2. Lately, his musical interests had expanded and he'd found a station on the radio that they called "classical music." It didn't have words to the songs, just instruments, but James enjoyed the musicians they referred to as, Mozart, Bach, and Beethoven, a name he found to be very funny, though he was incapable of laughing out loud.

"Errr?" James groaned and his mother knew he was asking the unspoken question, "*Where or what are we doing?*"

Alice Tramwell smiled down at her son, and said, "It's okay, James. We're going to get something to eat."

This made him feel better, but he was still intimidated by the sheer scale of the altar and the gigantic colored windows behind it. He began looking at the windows, even as they knelt down to receive the body of Christ. They seemed to be made up of tiny shards of colored glass and depicted scenes of Jesus, the man who his mother told him was "the Son of God." For some reason, long ago, they had killed Jesus and because of that, it made people better. It took away their "eternal sin." James didn't understand all that beyond the words, but he wondered why people who were supposed to love Jesus allowed Him to be killed, and in such a gruesome way: *nailed* to a cross. As he knelt at the altar, he wondered if they would kill him, too, and his heart began to beat faster.

Father MacMillan continued along the row of worshipers, and James could see he was placing a round, flat piece of bread in everyone's mouth. That would be okay, he supposed. He tilted his head back as he saw everyone else doing and waited his turn. But as he waited, he kept looking at the colored windows. They sparkled with the light that came through them and, after a while, it was all James could see…the light flashing: red, blue, yellow, green, flashing, flashing, *flashing*. James's eyelids began to flutter and suddenly his head felt like it was going to explode. There was an intense pain like he'd never felt before, and as Father MacMillan stood in front of him and said, "The body of Christ," the flashing colors in his head turned into a single bright light that ignited inside his brain. The bread went past his lips and James felt it stick to the roof of his mouth like a dry leech. He thought he would gag for a moment, but then everything went white, and his brain burned until he heard a popping sound, and then there was nothing else. There was not light, nor sounds, nor taste of bread in his mouth, and he felt himself falling, falling, then…nothing.

There was a sharp smell of *something*, it was like the liquid his mother cleaned the house with, the *ammonia*. It was a smell he did not like and he immediately opened his eyes. There was a man leaning over him, holding a white capsule-looking thing under his nose, and saying, "It's okay son, I'm a doctor. Are you okay?" And his mother was standing behind the doctor and holding her hand to her mouth, her eyes were filled with tears, and some ran down her cheeks. The scent of the ammonia seemed to sear into his already burning brain and caused his own eyes to water.

The doctor said, "You're okay James, you just had a little *seizure*." James was not sure what that meant, but he sat up. The dizziness began to fade as the doctor kept his fingers on James's wrist and looked at his watch. James remembered his own doctor telling him that was how they felt your heart beat.

Father MacMillan was explaining to the congregation that there had been a medical emergency and they were concluding a little early so they could attend to the matter. He blessed them all in the name of the Father, the Son, and the Holy Ghost. People began to shuffle out, staring at the boy lying on the floor in front of the altar and making the sign of the cross, or kissing their rosaries on the way by. The organist began playing music as the parishioners ambled out. He was playing Pachelbel's Canon.

As James listened to the music, the colors of the stained glass came back to his mind, but now they seemed like things he knew. They were organic, moving in patterns, and he could actually *see* the notes of the music and, with them, corresponding numbers. It all came to him in a rush that was both frightening and comforting, a confusing mesh that pushed a message from his brain down into his lungs and, finally, out of his mouth.

The doctor continued to fuss over him. But now, James became combative, and as the doctor tried to restrain him, he screamed out, "STOP!" The murmur from the departing crowd fell silent. Alice Tramwell and Father MacMillan genuflected.

Alice cried, "It's a miracle!" and fell to her knees, sobbing. It was the first word that had come from her son's mouth. MacMillan began to pray, looking up to the heavens. But they hadn't seen anything yet. The organist looked over his shoulder, but haltingly began to play again.

"Stop," said James again, this time calmer, quieter.

Now, the organist stopped playing and looked back at James, who was staring at him.

"Please," said James. "It…you…are playing it wrong." He walked forward, hesitantly at first, then with more conviction. He strode up the step of the altar and over to the alcove where the organ stood, now silent, and sat next to the organist. He placed his hands on the keys and, having never touched an instrument nor been trained in classical music, he began to play Pachelbel's Canon in D Major, perfectly.

His mother, already on her knees, now slumped to her side and fainted. Father MacMillan approached James, his hands trembling, his mouth working, trying to find the words. Then, he knelt behind him as James continued to play, and said, "Bless you, child. This is a miracle from God, and we are blessed to have seen it here in our church."

CHAPTER THREE

Present: Camp David

Camp David, formerly known as: the Naval Support Facility Thurmont, Catoctin Mountain Park, and, by at least one President, Shangri-La. Its exact location is not shown on any publicly available map. It has hosted every President since Franklin Roosevelt, as well as many foreign leaders, including Anwar Sadat, Menachem Begin, and Margaret Thatcher.

On this day, a group of the world's top scientists and political leaders, including the President of the United States and his staff, gathered to discuss a very grave matter. Addressing the group seated at an impossibly huge semi-circular table was Dr. Makiko Hisamoto. He was in his mid-eighties, but blessed with a still surprisingly dexterous mind. He was a world-renowned geophysicist.

President Jackson T. ("Tree Hugger") Cooper was listening intently to the discussion, his brow furrowed. A graduate of Harvard who studied philosophy before going to law school, Cooper had no scientific background. He was fifty-four years old and movie star handsome; a New England liberal in his third year in office. Formerly an attorney, he spent much of his professional time as an advocate who fought for ecological causes and organizations, such as the Nature Conservancy, Greenpeace, the National Wildlife Federation, and numerous other environmental protection agencies. When his opponent for the presidency called him a "tree hugger," he proudly made the supposedly derogatory comment his nickname and campaign slogan.

At his side was Vice President Stanley Proger, fifty-six years old. His crew cut looked like metal fragments stuck into his head and mowed with a diamond cut blade. He was a western conservative and former Secretary of Defense. Once a high ranking military officer, his first political seat was Governor of Nevada. He went on to become a U.S. Senator and once ran for President as an independent candidate. He was thought to be too moderate by his former Republican party, and his stances on pro-life and the right to bear arms was thought to be too conservative for the Democrats. Still, he was enormously popular with independent and libertarian voters, and his military background helped President Cooper establish his administration as "well-rounded," as well as bi-partisan. It was a brilliant pairing, but also a very radical idea for the President to construct, and one he hoped would finally unite the increasingly polarized parties for the first time since World War II.

"It is not accurate to say the nuclear detonation was not detected by the Vela project," said Hisamoto, his neck still showing the burn marks he sustained while a small child in Nagasaki, Japan. "It was." He looked around the room as if he were searching for someone to ease his burden of trying to explain the catastrophic event that was unfolding.

Gasps and whispered murmurings filled the room.

Hisamoto continued. "But, my understanding is that those who monitor the satellite images thought the characteristic footprint of the flashes could only have been a problem with the bhangmeters, as has been the case in the past." He spoke in English, though everyone was listening through headphones that translated words for those that desired to hear what was being said in their own language.

Dr. Erich Heimel, an Austrian nuclear scientist, seventy-three years old and also world-renown, interjected dryly, "The Vela Project was believed to have been abandoned over twenty years ago. Typically, with today's technology, we detect nuclear detonations using ARSA and RASA, the radioactive gas monitoring stations whose data collection center is located in Vienna. The problem is, unless it is surface detonation the gases may take weeks to be picked up by one of the sensors. The tell-tale signs of radioactive gases, such as xenon-133 or argon-37, may take from fifty to eighty days after detonation to seep into the atmosphere if the device was underground. If detonated at the bottom of the ocean, it could go undetected for months...."

Vice President Proger was visibly upset, his face red; his collar suddenly appeared to be too tight. "Who gives a flap doodle about any of that crap?" he heatedly interjected. "We know it was a nuclear device. Hell, it caused a foot-high tidal surge that almost flooded the southern states along the eastern seaboard, and the resultant fish kill was definitely from radiation. We're getting Geiger readings high enough for us to have closed the beaches throughout the Carolinas and Georgia."

"Excuse me, gentlemen," said President Cooper. "What is a bhangmeter, and who is responsible for monitoring the—what did you call it—Vela project?"

The scientists looked at each other worriedly, not sure which one should address the President. Finally, a bushy-haired man with intense dark eyes enlarged by thick lenses, Dr. Carl Edwards, an astrophysicist working with the Air Force, stood up sheepishly and cleared his throat. "Er...uh...bhangmeters, Mr. President, are the silicon photodiode sensors that are capable of monitoring light levels over sub-millisecond intervals. They are not very much different than the new adaptive optic lenses we are using in our Starfire Project, the...uh, laser-powered telescope project at Kirtland Air Force Base in New Mexico, though more primitive, of course." He reached into his coat pocket and withdrew a handkerchief and carefully, slowly, wiped the lenses of his glasses before continuing. "Still, they can detect a nuclear explosion within three thousand miles if they catch its unique signature: a short, intense flash, lasting about a millisecond, followed by a more prolonged but less intense emission of light. There is no natural phenomenon known that can produce this signature. And the answer to the second part of your questions is: we were. The United States originally funded the Vela project and are responsible for it, though the project has not been funded for some time..."

"Let's not start pointing fingers here," cautioned Proger. "We agreed our primary mission for meeting here today was to assess what we are going to do if the fault line continues to deteriorate, and find out who was responsible for setting off the damn bomb in the first place. Are they going to do it again? Was this an act of war? Me, I think it was the Greek terrorist group, known as 'November 17th.' The Greek economy is in an unprecedented state and what better way to bring attention to a country's plight than to explode a nuclear device?"

Homeland Security Director Alan Finney, a sixty-year-old former police chief from Los Angeles, with a shaved head and chiseled features, spoke up, "We think the device was detonated by age, actually, Mr. Vice President. Dr. Heimel, may I ask you to explain?"

Dr. Heimel stood up again, his oversized bow tie bobbing up and down on his Adam's apple like a ball caught in his throat. "The device was most likely designed to become thermo; that is, it contained a spark plug, if you will, filled with fusion fuel, most likely lithium-6 deuteride. This lithium is highly reactive to water. The bomb's casing deteriorated enough to allow sea water in, which reacted with the lithium and, in turn, detonated the bomb."

"Okay, okay, we got it," Proger said. "The damn thing went off, but where the hell did it come from?"

"You don't know, Mr. Vice President?" Heimel asked. "I'm surprised, given you used to be the Secretary of the Defense a couple of *regimes* ago. It is one of yours. Specifically, one of the *eleven* nuclear devices your armed forces managed to lose."

"Oh, to hell with that," said Proger, getting riled again. "Those idiotic myths have been floating around for years…"

"This one happens to be true," said Heimel, gaining confidence. "It is common knowledge among the scientific community that the Air Force jettisoned this bomb off the coast of Georgia some fifty years ago when a training mission was aborted after a mid-air collision. I cannot imagine who made the decision to leave a live nuclear bomb on a plane being used in a training mission, but, as the Vice President has said, we are not here to place blame, but to see what options we might have now. The bomb was an Mk-15, Model O, hydrogen bomb, one hundred times as powerful as the one used on Hiroshima," he paused long enough to throw a glance at Dr. Hisamoto, as if forcing him by sheer will to recall the devastation meted out to Japan. He continued, his face twisted, his tone sour, "It has probably been leaking radiation, contaminating the crab-fishing waters for years. What is not known is how the bomb managed to move so far out to sea, and so far to the north."

"Or why the Air Force never retrieved it…," said a voice from someone sitting three rows back.

A deafening silence engulfed the cavernous conference room. Looks were exchanged among the group as the general feeling in the room turned tense and fearful, trust began to dissipate from the room like an air freshener gone dry.

"If I may continue," said Dr. Hisamoto.

"Of course, doctor," said Cooper. He was the nation's peacekeeper and an ambassador to the world, a responsibility he never forgot, nor took lightly. He was exceedingly good at it and held the respect of the world like no president since Franklin Roosevelt. "Please. Stan, Alan, we'll work on the intelligence part later."

Dr. Hisamoto removed a remote device from his inside suit pocket and pointed to a bank of screens that was arranged in a semi-circle around the conference table. The image that emerged on the screen showed the ocean floor, its surface obviously uneven. A gigantic cliff was jutting up, its vertical surface crumbling even as the mass continued to grow in height.

Dr. Hisamoto continued, "My colleagues and I believe this is the scenario. This image you are viewing is a fault line along the continental shelf directly off the coast of Cape Hatteras. The tectonic plates that make up this structure have been shifting for years. It is possible that these shifts caused the bomb to move further out to sea slowly over the past fifty years. It was fortunate that the bomb moved away from the shoreline or the radioactive and explosive damage would have been much greater, as I'm sure Dr. Heimel can attest to. But, unfortunately, the bomb moved into such a position as to be lying along the edge of the tectonic plate that runs along the eastern seaboard. When it detonated, it created this vertical and escalating shelf that is, as you can see, deteriorating off Cape Hatteras. It is now evident that this fault line will fail, catastrophically, and very soon." Hisamoto paused for a moment, taking in an audible breath, then continued, "The failure will cause this massive shelf to fall, which you see being generated now, creating an enormous tsunami."

President Cooper had been glued to the screen, leaning forward, his hand unconsciously placed over his mouth. He removed his hand, and asked, "How big of a tidal wave are we talking about, Dr. Hisamoto?"

Hisamoto's eyes blinked rapidly, appearing wet and shining. "I'm afraid it will be the largest tidal wave to ever hit the North American continent." He paused, swallowing, then continued, "We estimate it will be some sixty to one hundred feet high, worse, it will be widespread. We think twice, perhaps three times the spread of the tsunami that struck Indonesia in 2004, and perhaps ten times the size of the one that struck Japan after the Tohuku quake in 2011. As you are aware, the secondary damage from the destruction of the three nuclear facilities exacerbated the catastrophe. Currently, the United States has one hundred and four nuclear plants. Over half of them are in the anticipated path of this tidal wave. They are not expected to withstand its forces."

The images on the screen changed to show the eastern coast of the United States taken from a satellite. A red overlay showed the approximate area of the projected tsunami strike. Dr. Hisamoto continued, "We believe the tsunami wave will extend as far north as New York and as far south as Florida. In other words, the entire east coast will be negatively impacted. The Gulf Coast states, even as far as Louisiana and Texas will be flooded. Some states, particularly Florida and all of the low lying coastal areas will be...completely submerged, at least for a while."

For a moment nothing was said, as a shaken Dr. Hisamoto looked nervously around the room. He seemed afraid to mention one last thing. "The radioactive fallout will be widespread due to the tidal flooding. The affected area will be...unlivable for perhaps a century, or more."

"That's a grim forecast, Dr. Hisamoto," said President Cooper. "Have all of your colleagues agreed on such a negative projection?"

"Yes, sir. We, the scientific community and I, have also agreed that...eh..."

"Yes?" prompted the President. "What else have you agreed on?"

Hisamoto looked around the room again, as if seeking help. "That there is nothing we can do to stop it."

"I see," said Cooper.

He got up from his seat and went to the window where he stood grasping his chin in his hand. Acid poured into his stomach, just as it would to any person under stress. But, in his case, there could be no relief, no one to share the burden of his responsibility. Images of faces, persons he'd met as the leader of the free world, and when he was campaigning for this thankless position, flashed through his head so quickly it almost made him dizzy. Farmers, bus drivers, café owners, retired men and women, cops, fire fighters, small business and giant corporation owners, cab drivers, small town mayors, sports giants and little league players, teachers and professors, students, linemen, pipe layers, carpenters, plumbers, and homeless veterans; in short, every type of American citizen, as well as those who were not yet citizens. He owed an immeasurable debt to each and every one. There were no days off, no down time, and no one to whom he could pass the buck. It was all *him*.

As he stared through the window, the President of the United States watched a flock of birds flying, his ears ringing from the pressure in the room. He could smell the body sweat, the scent of aftershaves and perfumes and deodorant. The scent of smoke from the tobacco users. The smell of fear from everyone. He could smell his own skin, feel the stubble forming on his neck, his humanness, his own weakness to be able to fix this problem. He swallowed, and it was dry and painful, like eating a sandspur followed by heartburn. He didn't know what he was looking for, but he kept watching the birds as they flew in a distinct V-shaped pattern. This comforted him for reasons he was not aware of; his breathing and heart rate slowed.

Nervous murmuring filled the room and grew louder the longer he stood there, but he absorbed this tiny slice of peace. Finally, he turned and addressed the assembly, his countenance firm.

"I almost wish this was a terrorist attack. At least it would make sense to America. How can I explain to our good citizens that this disaster has been caused by a bomb that we lost, then…then, what?" His eyes gleamed with subtle anger. "Were we too lazy to look for it? God help us. Alan, are the polls showing that the media believes what the Press Secretary told them?"

"Yes, sir," said Finney. "For now. We're holding to the story that the explosion is of unknown origin, but we believe it to be a gigantic undersea volcano that erupted. The only media reporting evidence of radiation has been the tabloids...but we have another story about a meteorite striking that area that could explain the increased radioactive levels."

Cooper's mouth was a flat line, the edges turned down in disgust. "That won't last long. I'm surprised the New York Times hasn't sent someone down with a Geiger counter already." After a moment, he added, "Damn it! I hate deceiving the public, but it seems we have few choices here. What about our mitigation, our contingencies?"

Finney stood up again, fatigue settling across his face like a weighted shadow as he delivered his bleak forecast. "As Dr. Hisamoto said, sir. Nothing can stop it. We can start evacuations all along the eastern seaboard but frankly, sir, we're at a loss as to how that would turn out. Where would millions, tens of millions of people go? This would not be a short term evac. Where would they live? There's no way we can house that many people or even come close to these numbers. What do they do now for work? Their businesses—entire communities—will be lost. Banks closed. How do we transport that many people? Is there enough fuel stored to allow that kind of mass migration? We'd have to use the entire might of our armed forces with this endeavor, and they would be spread so thin their efficacy would be questionable. The aftermath of Katrina showed us there will undoubtedly be widespread panic that would lead to random acts of violence and crime, looting, fuel and food hoarding. The economy will be destroyed in America as well as all those countries that depend on us. It would, rather quickly, affect the whole world."

Dr. Heimel stood again and addressed the group, "We've estimated the debris field which will, ahem," he cleared his throat before continuing, "also contain unsustainable levels of radiation. It will be larger than the Gulf of Mexico and will negatively affect the coastline of Central and South America almost immediately before reaching the shores of Europe and Northern Africa, perhaps within weeks, if not days."

Cooper paced the room, aggressively now, his arms crossed, deep in thought. Like any other man, he thought about his family. His wife was probably out visiting schools that were well within the path of potential destruction. His son had just begun classes at Harvard, which was also in the danger zone. His daughter, born deaf, was probably working with her speech therapist at the White House. His stomach clenched when he realized she would never even hear emergency sirens if they went off. He struggled to keep his mind clear and on the nation's needs more than his own. He once believed in miracles, but not at this moment.

Secretary of State Michelle Badgewell, a distinguished woman in her mid-forties, shoulder length hair flipped up on the ends like a model from a shampoo commercial, interrupted his thoughts, "There *has* to be something. I'd be willing to hear anything, even a non-traditional...crazy idea...at this point. In this room, we have assembled perhaps the greatest scientific minds in history. Haven't any of you thought of *something* we can do to counter this?"

Dr. Hisamoto looked around the room, but it was a perfunctory exercise; he and his colleagues had already poured over the problem, night and day, since they were first made aware of it forty-eight hours ago. "This is a global incident that has never been encountered in our recorded history, Secretary Badgewell. Truthfully, there is *nothing* that can be done."

"You have a valid point, Dr. Hisamoto," said the President. "I assume that is why the suggestion was made by the scientific community to keep the truth from the media?"

"That's partly correct, Mr. President. We were concerned about how this would affect the civilian population, globally. But, also, we were not sure how bad the situation was until some of our field people visited the site."

Hisamoto clicked his remote and changed the picture on the screen again. This time a video was projected showing the fault line, a huge crack caving in, growing not by inches but by feet, like a giant laceration in the skin of the earth that was ripping open.

Cooper moved to the window again, staring out as if hoping he might find an answer beyond the confines of the room; there were none *in* the room. It was a beautiful pastoral day, the sky as blue as a baby's bonnet, cotton ball clouds drifted by, almost skimming the tops of the evergreen canopy that surrounded the compound. It was as if nothing were wrong in the world. And again, the birds. Starlings, the President thought, flew by, in a semi-circle this time.

Then a bee landed on the window and began frantically moving in a continuous circle. The President frowned as he watched it. A light sweat shined his forehead. "We'll need some further analysis, at the very least," he said, almost absently.

"It is your prerogative, Mr. President," said Hisamoto. "But there is nothing, physically, or scientifically, that can be done to stop this…incident. It would be like trying to stop a Category 5 hurricane or, well, an earthquake." He dabbed the burn scar on his neck with a handkerchief.

Cooper turned from the window, his face stern. "I understand and appreciate your candor, Dr. Hisamoto. But I was thinking more along the lines of forecasting how the event will affect those who are most threatened by it and what we can expect on a mass behavioral standpoint from those whom we assume will survive. In other words, we're going to have to have some strong ideas about how we're going to deal with a recovery effort and what type of mass mentality we'll be coping with. Alan?"

"Yes, sir?"

"Can you locate Dr. Stephen Pevnick for me?"

Finney frowned and twisted his mouth, rubbed his neck, searching his memory for the name. "The behavioral specialist who worked with us last year on the National Emergency Plan?"

"Yes, that's him." Cooper maintained his professional countenance, but in truth, he and Stephen Pevnick had grown to be friends when the scientist worked with his administration as an advisor on the new emergency plan. He knew him to be brilliant, methodical, but also intuitive. He needed a man like him right now. A man he could trust. A man with no agenda except to try to help people and bridge the gaps of misunderstanding.

"Should be able to," Finney stated. "Last I knew, he was beginning to work on another project. Something to do with… retarded people, I think…"

Dr. Hisamoto interrupted, "Savants, sir. Not retarded, nor Down's syndrome patients. Savants are persons with…extraordinary abilities."

Everyone in the room turned their attention to Hisamoto, as he continued, "I know of his project because he has borrowed, if you will, Japan's most famous savant, Etta Kim. She's a prodigious savant whose unique ability is designing things—engineering, I suppose you could say, though not in a traditional manner."

"That will have to wait, I'm afraid," said Cooper. "Alan, get hold of him. Immediately. Tell him we need him for some analysis on a project of the utmost importance to national, even international, security."

"What if he's not available, sir?"

Cooper cocked his head to one side as if he couldn't believe the question. He wanted to convey the importance of bringing the man on board, but not reveal their friendship. In spite of the new transparency of government, it was not always a good or safe thing to reveal friendships. They could be compromised.

"The last I knew he lived on the east coast, near the shore in Maine," said Cooper. "If he shows any reluctance, tell him the truth. That might serve as a motivator for him. Maine might not get the full assault of the wave, but I am sure it will be negatively affected. Dr. Hisamoto, how much time do you think we have? I know it's difficult to project with accuracy, but what's your gut telling you?"

"We've calculated the growth of the fault line. It's growing at a measurable pace right now. We, the majority of the scientific community and I, believe we have another week, give or take a day. But, sir, I emphasize again, no one can be sure. The fissure is similar to the west coast San Andreas Fault, only less stable. In other words, it could go at any time. Please don't blame me if it goes sooner..."

"Blame you?" replied Cooper. "If it goes, I'll be dead along with a third of America's population. Let's get started, people. Dr. Hisamoto, Dr. Heimel, I thank you and your colleagues for your presentation. Department Directors, I appreciate you being here. Go back to your departments and start making preparations for evacuations—that will be on my order only—as best you can. Tell them we are implementing a large scale practice of the National Emergency Plan we designed last year. We'll need to get the UN involved, but we need to try to keep a lid on this for a couple more days. If the truth gets out, we should downplay the validity and/or severity of the problem until we can get a better handle on what our emergency and recovery plans are going to be. Everyone in this room has our top security clearance. Please don't forget that. If we are to be successful at all, it will be due to our trust and cooperation with each other. Is that understood?"

All heads in the room nodded in solemn agreement.

The President continued, "Stan, inform the rest of the cabinet and let's get every available member of the armed forces headed toward the east coast. Keep minimal staffing levels at our far western bases; California and Hawaii, particularly. Bring them east. Let's make Ft. Benning in Georgia our staging area in the south. It'll be close enough for deployment to the most affected areas but should be far enough inland in case the event is premature. We'll make this camp the northern staging area and use the National Fire Academy for overflow. Close all National Parks that used to be military bases and let's see what it would take to bring them back on line as such. This takes absolute priority. Start repositioning all state-side National Guard and Army reserves along the eastern seaboard in case we move ahead with the evacuations. Everything else is on hold for now."

"I'll take responsibility for all military actions and planning, sir," Vice President Proger offered.

"Right," said Cooper. "Alan, get your departments ready for mass migration planning. Try to anticipate every contingency and problem: communications is number one. Fuel, food, housing, everything we've talked about previously only on a bigger scale, comes after that. Get with the Departments of Housing, Commerce, Federal Reserve…hell, get with everybody and brief them. Start lining up emergency funding and all associated logistics. But stress this: no media contact. Madam Secretary, you will handle all international inquiries with the message we will have established by this afternoon and by which we will all maintain for consistency. Nationally, everything goes through the Press Secretary from me or, in my stead, Vice President Proger."

He turned to the rest of the group and addressed them:

"Ladies and gentlemen, you all know the severity of this situation. It's like nothing we've ever encountered before. Let's make a pact, here and now, that we'll share all knowledge. Don't stop working on this, no matter how futile it seems. If you think of something, anything at all that might help us mitigate this event or assist with a rapid and orderly recovery, put it on the table. Nothing is off limits as far as ideas go. My staff will field and assess incoming ideas, but I will retain constant vigilance on this matter, and you will have personal access to me if you have any plans that might help us. Let's put away any political differences we might have and reinforce those relationships and agreements that will help us produce a better outcome when this event occurs. Now, let's pray."

President Cooper's words were strong and encouraged agreement with everyone present. Scientists and political leaders nodded, then bowed their heads, but most of them had the same self-preserving thought: *where can I go to be as far away from here as possible?*

CHAPTER FOUR

In the Beehive, the group assembled in the library.

The room's walls were paneled mahogany on top of burgundy-striped wainscoting, positioned over a woodsy green carpet that felt like the lush moss floor of a forest. Etta, the demure girl from Japan, had slipped off her shoes and was burying her toes into the carpet.

Dr. Pevnick gathered together the group of so-called savants, a task that had taken him close to three years to get permission from those in charge of their care; parents, physicians, psychologists, as well as the legal twists and turns, travel arrangements, and the biggest hurdle—convincing a bunch of extraordinary people that it would be in their own and the world's best interest to allow him to study them as a group. None of them had siblings, or any close friends other than those caretakers responsible for their well-being. To most of them the idea was as foreign an idea as interplanetary travel. Most of them had never set foot outside of their hometowns. After a couple days to make them feel more comfortable, Pevnick asked them all to come to his study for the first time to explain his project to them as a group.

Pevnick looked around the room smiling benignly, his eyes almost wet with emotion. If he could not succeed beyond this simple gathering, he told himself, it was still an achievement. But he wondered with unbridled anticipation, what could they do together? What could he, and possibly the world, learn?

To his immediate right sat James Tramwell, who, in spite of

being dressed for several hours now, was still silently counting his clothes, his hands under the table as they drifted over his garments while his lips silently mouthed: *one, two, three...*

To James's right was Jeremy Clemens. He was eighteen years old, black, and a rather large young man who looked more like a middleweight boxer than a sculptor. He was wearing underwear— no pants—that were neatly pressed, calf-length white crew socks with penny loafers that actually had pennies in them, and a black, knit pullover that made him look like a French underground resistance fighter caught in a wardrobe change. His "gifts" were the ability to accurately sculpt anything he saw or could think of, as well as "perfect appreciation," the ability to tell time at any moment, anywhere in the world. His biggest hurdle was that he was echolalic, repeating words and phrases so often it typically rendered his speech unintelligible and confusing. Most people gave up the attempt after a few moments, including his parents, so that his total experience with meaningful dialogue had been less in his entire life than most people experienced in a week.

Continuing to the right, there was Harvey Peet. He was twenty years old, Australian, and the oldest in the group. He was heavy set and wore thick glasses like James, though he preferred tortoise-shell frames, which were held together with a piece of silver duct tape. His head was large, almost mushrooming at the top due to his oversized brain, an organ that was an anomaly in itself as it did not contain the septum, the dividing membrane of the two halves of the normal brain. His eyes constantly scanned back and forth horizontally, so that it appeared he was watching something run by him, again and again. This aberration was actually part of his gift, which was the ability to read with almost lightning speed and remember *everything* he read. He could answer every question posed to him on any subject, including dates, the day of the week, persons involved, geographic locations, etcetera. His passion was anything to do with science. His hurdle was that he was a coprolalic, cussing uncontrollably like someone with Tourette's syndrome. He had been trained to deal with this and knew it was socially unacceptable, so he tried to use various nonsense words to mask this affliction. Lately, he had been endeavoring to use the word, *cuss*, rather than actually use a curse word. It was distracting, but certainly more socially acceptable. His clothes were disheveled and his hair constantly askew, as if the wind was his personal mad stylist.

Lastly, there was Etta Kim from Japan. She was the youngest at seventeen. She was small in stature, truly a porcelain doll, and painfully quiet. Her features were small—specifically her nose, mouth and ears, but her eyes were too big for her tiny face, giving the overall impression of a nocturnal creature caught in the light. Her hair was long, black and cut as evenly as if a machine had trimmed it. She sat ramrod-straight, impeccably clothed in a dress that looked like it was made for a child. Her gift was an innate sense of engineering, the ability to design and draw, in three-dimension and to scale, anything she could imagine, some of which was inexplicable machinery and imaginary underwater cities. She told people these things were "from memory." Her hurdle was that she displayed "stimming," an uncontrollable movement of her hands and arms, which grew worse when she was nervous, but ceased completely when she drew a picture or was in close proximity to the sea or its abundant life.

"We've all had a few days to get acquainted," began Pevnick, in an attempt to break the ice. "I trust everyone is comfortable..."

"Some of us, crap...I mean, *cccrrruuudd, hellllll, hel-per... unicorn...cuss, cuss...*more than others," said Harvey, his constantly scanning eyes locking in on Jeremy.

Jeremy replied, "I am, how you say, a-wake from I hear Harvey, snoring and farting in his sleep, *oui?* Snoring and farting, snoring and farting."

Harvey smiled proudly and took a little bow, a gesture that elicited quiet titters from the group.

Pevnick smiled and resisted the temptation to correct them on social niceties. "What about you, Etta? Are you comfortable?" he asked.

Etta's hands were folded, but once the attention turned to her she became visibly nervous. Her hands went rigid and started flapping, which traveled up through her arms, and she began to jerk chaotically.

Pevnick anticipated this happening and quickly reached into his inside coat pocket and withdrew a starfish. "I found this on the shore a few days ago. It was already dead or I would have thrown it back in the ocean. I thought you might like it," he said, and placed it on the table in front of her.

Etta's arms came to rest at her side and her hands softened and calmed as she picked up the starfish, as if seeing one for the first time. She ran her fingers over the animal's bumpy skin, her fingers touching it so delicately it was as if she believed it would shatter.

"I...am...comfortable. Thank you, Dr. Pevnick," she said, without making eye contact with anyone in the group.

"You're welcome, Etta. Now then, I told you all a few days ago that our goal here is for all of us, eh...that is *you*, to try to work on a common problem. All of you have such diverse talents I thought it best if I picked the project. I hope you don't mind."

They all looked at each other briefly, and shook their heads.

"Let's fu...fu...*fruitcake*...sorry...hear it," said Harvey, his face flushed with the exertion of trying not to use profanity. None of the others seemed to notice, or if they did, they didn't show it.

"Very well," said Pevnick. "I chose a project that is nothing new, technologically, but it is something none of you have worked on previously on your own."

James cocked his head to one side and said, dryly, "The suspense is killing me, Dr. Pevnick."

"I want you to work on a solar-powered device." Pevnick looked around at the group to note their reactions, his Steno pad close by. There was little to no reaction except from James, who shook his head and smiled. "You disapprove, James?"

"No. I just thought it would be something more...difficult."

"Well, it would be for me. I wouldn't have an idea where to start. And, it won't be that easy for you. First, you have to agree on what it is you want to build—I'm only giving you the parameters that it has to be solar-powered. Second, you will have to research and design it. And, third, whatever it is, you will have to make it from scratch. All the tools and materials you will need are housed in a machinist's shop located just down the road on this property. Anything else you discover you need, you will have to order. It might sound easy, as you say, but every step of the project will have its challenges. Your ability to overcome those challenges is all part of my research."

James looked at Etta and realized she might not understand

everything that was being said. In anticipation of meeting her, he'd learned her language, and as Pevnick spoke, he translated the gist of the conversation to her. Then, he turned to Jeremy and did the same thing in French. It was, perhaps, the first time in his life that he had done something for someone else. It was a socialization skill, a subtle one, but it did not go unnoticed by Dr. Pevnick, who jotted down some notes. James turned back to him and nodded, announcing he was done.

"Thank you, James. That was most helpful," said Pevnick. He looked at the others around the table. "So, you see, there will be challenges."

No one responded initially and the silence was disquieting, then Jeremy spoke up, "Your watch is losing time, Dr. Pevnick, losing time, losing time..."

Dr. Pevnick looked at his watch, curious. "Oh, I don't think so, Jeremy. This is a very fine watch. A Rolex. The best there is. In fact, it was given to me by the President of the United States." He said this as a way of affirmation and not braggadocio.

His secretary, Mrs. Olivia Brown, came into the room carrying a portable phone. She was an older woman, her grey-streaked hair pulled into a tight bun; her collar buttoned high, her stature as straight as a colonial chair. Her attire was always professional, typically Ann Taylor, though on a whim she might wear J Crew or some other tasteful choice. She was all business in spite of her kind and still pretty face. Her assistance to Dr. Pevnick was constant and invaluable.

"I'm sorry to bother you, doctor, but you have an urgent phone call..."

Pevnick glanced at his watch again; a habit he had developed so that when he took notes, he had the time marked next to each one. He saw his watch had stopped. He frowned and looked up at Jeremy, his mouth slightly agape in surprise.

"I can fix eet for you, monsieur...zee watch. Fix eet for you. Eet should read 1:11pm. Eet ees also 7:11 in Budapest and 9:11 in Anchorage."

Pevnick slipped off his watch and absent-mindedly handed it to Jeremy. "Who is it, Mrs. Brown?" the doctor asked his secretary. "I'd rather not be disturbed right now."

Mrs. Brown tilted her head up slightly. "It's the *President*, sir."

"Of the United States?"

"Yes. That one."

Pevnick looked confused for a moment. He was not a superstitious man, but the timing of the failure of his watch—the one given to him by the President—and the President calling him at the same time was, to say the least, strange. He took a deep breath, looked around the table apologetically, and accepted the phone from Mrs. Brown.

"Do you believe in coincidences, Dr. Pevnick?" asked James.

Pevnick shook his head, his hand over the phone.

"You should, doctor," James advised. "Coincidences are mathematically provable. They aren't really miracles, you know. I can show you, but the numbers can be quite…long."

"Later, James," said Pevnick, whispering. He turned to the rest of the group, "Excuse me. Please, all of you. I have to take this phone call."

The group—the *savants*—didn't seem to mind. They began to mill about the room, which was filled with shelves of books. Without conversation, they individually began to pull out some of the volumes and started thumbing through them. Except for Jeremy, who found a letter opener in the room and was using it to pry open the casing to Pevnick's Rolex.

They were all quick readers, but Harvey read so quickly, it was almost comical. He turned pages so fast, it was as if he was making a joke; he couldn't possibly be capturing the words much less retaining the book's information, but he *was*. He smiled and adjusted his crotch absently and repeatedly as he absorbed the text. No one else seemed to mind, but Mrs. Brown frowned at him and tightened her mouth in disapproval. Harvey noticed and winked at her.

"This is Dr. Pevnick," he addressed the caller, just as Jeremy dropped the watch's delicate inner mechanisms all over the floor.

"*Sacre bleu!*" said Jeremy. "*Sacre…sacre…*"

James acted as if he were helping to pick up the pieces of the disassembled watch, but he watched, listening closely to Pevnick as he spoke to the President. James did not believe in coincidences.

Pevnick's eyes went wide, but he was, obviously, obligated to learn what the President wanted. "Er, uh...hello. Yes, sir. I am well. How are you, Mr. President? Yes. Uh-huh. Well, no, sir. I have not checked my messages today. No, I didn't know Director Finney was trying to reach me. No. But...yes. I've been working on a research project involving several subjects that have come from all over the world and...yes. I understand. Of course. Very well. I'll...see you shortly."

Pevnick hung up the phone and looked at the group. "The President will be here in a few minutes. I'm sorry...but, I'll have to...excuse myself. We will get back to, uh...the project shortly."

"He wants to talk to you about the end of the world," said James, matter–of–fact, flipping through a post graduate studies book on partial differential equations as if he was reading something as simple as a comic book.

"Why would you say such a thing, James?" asked Pevnick.

James did not take his eyes off the book, but addressed the question, "Remember what I said about coincidences? This is not a coincidence; the President coming here, this group assembled."

Cars were heard pulling up the crushed rock drive outside. Heavy doors opened and shut. Pevnick got up and went to the window of the study. A procession of black, unmarked federal cars were pulling in. Secret Service agents piled out of the cars and began fanning out across the property, talking on small communication devices attached to their wrists, sunglasses glinting. They did a complete three-sixty of the compound before allowing the President's car to approach. When the town car he was riding in did come up the drive, it was flanked by agents in dark suits.

President Cooper stepped out of one side of the car and Homeland Security Director Finney appeared from the other side.

James stepped up next to Dr. Pevnick and gazed out the window, his hands in his pockets. "I repeat, this is not a coincidence, Dr. Pevnick."

"You're mistaken, James. The President's visit has nothing to do with our project."

"A higher power has brought us together," said James, mechanically. "I'm not attempting to make you believe in some paranormal gibberish. I'm stating a fact. And, I'm telling you, even miracles have mathematical probabilities. The number of sperm that try to reach the egg and only one of them, a special one, is allowed into the egg to create the miracle of life. That is a mathematical equation whether you subscribe to miracles or not."

"It's biology, James. Science could show you how, and probably why, that one sperm made it into that egg."

Harvey bulled his way in between the two men at the window, his eyes spanning back and forth like a railroad crossing warning. "Are we going to meet the fu…fu…*frigging* President? Been wanting to say something to him for years."

Pevnick placed his hand on Harvey's shoulder. "Yes, Harvey. You get to meet the President. But, maybe you should let me do the talking for now. Okay?"

CHAPTER FIVE

Dr. Pevnick stepped out onto the front gallery to meet President Cooper and his entourage of Finney and several Secret Service men. Mrs. Brown stood by discreetly. Cooper pulled ahead of his group and energetically mounted the steps leading up to the gallery, his hand extended. He was wearing a white, pressed shirt, sleeves rolled up, his blue-striped tie loose, no jacket, navy pants over black, laced-up shoes. He looked tired.

"Stephen, good to see you again," he said.

"Well, it's wonderful to see you again, Mr. President," said Pevnick.

"I'm sorry to barge in on you, but when I tell you what brought me here, you'll understand my urgency."

"Of course, sir. Please, come in. Can I have Mrs. Brown bring you anything?"

"That would be nice, you know I love her sweet tea if she has some made."

"Just made some a half-hour ago, along with some homemade oatmeal raisin cookies," said Mrs. Brown, stepping around Dr. Pevnick.

The President took her hand and gave a slight nod. "Hi, Mrs. Brown. You're looking well."

Mrs. Brown blushed as most women did who met him. "Oh, thank you. And how is the First Lady?"

"She's well, thank you," said President Cooper. "She'd be jealous if she knew I was here right now getting ready to chow down on your famous cookies. I could smell them coming up the drive."

"You're too kind. Please come in and I'll bring your refreshments to Dr. Pevnick's office."

One of the Secret Service men stepped up to the President. "Excuse me, sir. Do you mind if we go ahead of you and do a quick check?"

Cooper placed his hand on the agent's shoulder and smiled. "Thank you, Smitty. But Dr. Pevnick is a friend of mine."

"But, sir…"

Pevnick stepped in. "It's okay, Mr. President. I'd rather everyone feel safe where you're concerned. Come in, Agent Smith. Mrs. Brown can give you a quick tour…then bring the President and I some refreshments. Is that okay with you, Mrs. Brown?"

"Of course, sir."

The group moved forward and into the home; the agents moved ahead quickly, efficiently, and quietly. Cooper and Pevnick sought out the doctor's office, one agent silently following them. Director Finney stayed outside on the gallery, constantly making and receiving calls.

Inside, the smell of warm cinnamon greeted President Cooper and gave him a feeling of well-being and comfort; the first he'd had since being briefed on the situation two days ago. It brought back memories of childhood, of family and good times and no worries, of playing on the beach in the summer and in the piles of fallen, golden leaves in the autumn. While so many people thought they'd like to have his job, the fact was, it is the most trying position in the world. Cooper thrived on its challenges, but he would not recommend it to anyone. It aged a person, and he knew it had him. He suddenly felt weary, the kind of fatigue that envelops a traveler after they finally make it home.

Inside the office, Pevnick insisted on the President taking his own overstuffed leather chair, it's brass buttoned surface worn to a perfect level of comfort, if not beauty, while he sat in a more practical chair across from him. They threw some chit-chat back and forth until Mrs. Brown delivered the tea and cookies and departed the room. Cooper's face grew somber, his tone like that of someone preparing to deliver a eulogy.

"Stephen," began Cooper, "What I am going to share with you is extremely sensitive."

"Of course, Mr. President. I assume any time you have to make an emergency stop at my home…"

"Please, call me Jack," the President interrupted. "With what I'm going to tell you, I think we can drop some formalities."

"Okay…Jack. Is this a personal matter? If it is, I can assure you any counseling you might be considering would be confidential. I don't even have to take notes…"

Cooper smiled, briefly, at the suggestion. "It's not that, Stephen, but thanks. I'll keep it in mind. It's certainly something I'll consider if I, *we*, can get through this…well, I'll just tell you what *it* is." He paused, turning to look out the window of the office as if it might be the last time he'd see the ocean, this beautiful place.

"The nation is on the verge of…a disaster, unparalleled in our history," Cooper said. "There is a fault line that is failing along the eastern coast of the United States. It's creating an underwater land mass that will, eventually—and very soon—collapse. I'm told it is inevitable and unstoppable. The shift will result in a massive tidal wave that will engulf most of the eastern seaboard. Casualty predictions and impact to businesses and communities are already projected. Within a very short while, we will begin to evacuate entire states. Of course, you can speculate the panic and chaos that most Americans will succumb to. We are exploring every contingency and mitigation effort. We have the best scientists in the world working on this, but the forecast is bleak, as you can imagine."

"My God…Jack," Dr. Pevnick tried to consider the unbelievable pressure the man sitting across from him must be under; it was his instinct to do so. He still believed that Cooper was discussing this problem as part of a personal revelation, a cathartic process he must pass through in order to help stabilize his decisions. "What can I do for you?"

"Not me, Stephen. The country. What I need you to do is some analysis; a psychological projection, if you will, of what will happen to…our people. I'm sorry to drop this responsibility on you like this, but none of us have the luxury of choice, or etiquette, right now. You're the most qualified man I know who can assess the mass behavioral predictions, and I need to make a decision on the evacuation and relocation of literally tens of millions of people."

"Sir, I'm flattered, but other than the advisory work I've done with your Department of Homeland Security on rare occasions, I don't have a lot of experience with emergency preparedness."

"This is no time to be modest, Stephen. I have people trained and knowledgeable in emergency preparedness, mitigation, and recovery. They know the logistics: how much food and water ten thousand, a hundred thousand, or a million people can consume; the number of vehicles and shelters needed to move and house entire communities. But, there are few people who can predict what kind of behaviors we can expect, other than anecdotal and historical models."

Pevnick leaned forward in his chair, unconsciously rubbing his hand over his face and up through his thick, unruly hair. "I understand and appreciate your confidence in me, Jack. I'll get to work on it immediately, of course. I'll need at least twenty-four hours, more if possible. It's going to be a rough draft at best, but I'll try to make predictions based on the disaster data we compiled the last several years. The Katrina experience will help as a base of knowledge, I should think. The Malaysian tsunami, too, and certainly Japan's disaster, which would include the secondary nuclear power plants' crisis. I could expand, adding exponential quotients, then make some speculations. You'd have to realize that… it would be speculative at best."

Cooper smiled warmly, sipping sweet tea and nibbling at a still warm cookie. "Your speculations are more accurate than most science-backed theories I'm aware of. If we would have used the model you wrote about in your thesis twenty years ago, we would've had a better outcome in Louisiana and Mississippi, as well as those places in the Midwest affected by the number of tornadoes last year. We could have handled the aftermath of 9/11 better. We were reactive rather than proactive. We can't operate like that anymore. I'm looking for some justification to uproot the entire eastern seaboard, then integrate those people into other cities and towns without disrupting those unaffected areas, too. I don't want to place burden and hardships on those people who are lucky enough to survive. I've got scores of people working on the economic impacts, logistics, and contingencies. What I need from you is a sociological forecast, short and long term, if possible."

Pevnick had begun to consider the enormity of the task and had let his mind wander. Projections of an apocalyptic world filled with people who had turned to savagery from hunger and thirst oozed into his mind, like a memory of a plague that leveled the medieval era. He felt his stomach churn with anxiety but he took a deep breath and tried to show the confidence he knew the President expected of him.

"I'll do my best, sir, but you know disaster outcomes are nearly as impossible to predict as the disasters themselves."

"You were right on the money with your predictions for Katrina, Stephen. No one else was. Your work on the National Emergency Plan was solid, too, but it's still not on the scale of what this event will be. I'll need you to be just as sharp on this. Of course, I know it's unprecedented. Do the best you can. That's all—and everything— any of us can do anymore."

"I'll need access to the logistical stats you were talking about, primarily to get some numbers, and full demographic city-by-city information."

"We've already anticipated that. I've talked to my staff and you have the highest security clearance for anything you need. The Defense Department will have the logistics. The Census Bureau should be able to give you demographics. Your contact will be Alan Finney, the Director of Homeland Security. He's juggling two jobs right now since my Chief of Staff, Ken Fontana, passed last week."

"I'm sorry, sir," said Pevnick. "I heard the news stories about that. A heart attack, was it?"

"Yes. Unbelievable. Ken was in remarkable shape, avid cyclist and runner, always hiking or boating with his family. He was ten years younger than me and…irreplaceable. I've been at wits end without him. Alan agreed to double duty until I can find a replacement, but this crisis has kept me too busy to even think about that right now. He's outside making phone calls and covering my backside right now, but he gave me this Blackberry to give you. It has all the phone numbers and contacts you'll need, my cabinet, and every department director there is. If there's something, or someone you need that's not on there, call him and he'll take care of it. Do you remember Alan?"

"Sure do. He's a sharp guy."

"He's available twenty-four-seven for you. We all are. This is a team effort. None of us goes home or sleeps until we have some handle on this...situation." Cooper paused as he stood and once more, caught himself drawn to a window. It dawned on him that the outdoors, even when separated from him by a pane of glass, gave him strength and comfort.

"Stephen," the President continued, "I know you'll do a professional report, even with the time constraints. But, personally, I'll want to know a few things outside of a report I'll have to give to Congress. First, I want to know how this thing, in all probability, will affect the nation's psyche. Will we pull together to endure a common crisis, or become a nation of desperate and warring bands of savages killing each other for a foot of higher ground? Second, I want to know how John Q. Citizen from Manhattan might react when he is permanently displaced, jobless, and living with a group of blue collar workers in portable housing in Farmland, U.S.A., and vice versa. Can we move rural folks into the cities? Try to think of all the diverse cultures pushed together. And lastly, please, for me, try to think: are there any words of strength I can offer the nation, to try to prepare them for what is going to happen?" Cooper paused, then added, "What grain of hope can we give them to endure?"

Pevnick pondered the request for several moments before answering. "I'm no speech writer," he said, finally, "but I think I know what you're looking for. I'll do my best. Some of it will be educated hunches." Again he considered the enormity of the situation and the pressure the President must be under. His interest was always in behavioral science, but he was also a licensed psychiatrist. He felt compelled to offer some solace to the President, but could not find the words. "I...can't believe this is happening, sir."

"That's expected and understood, Stephen." He placed his hand on Dr. Pevnick's shoulder, knowing what he was trying to do. But as the President, he also knew he must live with the responsibility that came with this job, and that was often a lonely task by its very nature.

Pevnick stood, and the two men shook hands, looking at each other's face for what may be the last time. The gravity of the situation was so final, so uncompromising, that to continue a discussion seemed like a waste of precious time.

"Well," Cooper announced, "I should be going."

"Could you do me one small favor before you leave, Jack?" Pevnick asked hesitantly.

"Sure. What is it?"

"Say hello to some very special people?"

"Of course. Are these the savants Alan told me about? By the way, is that the correct word for them?"

"Yes, sir. They know they are different; they have been diagnosed by their own doctors and have come to terms with their differences. I appreciate you asking, though."

"Sure. I wish they had some protocols for this type of thing. I mean, common sense nowadays tells you we should refer to Down's as just that, but I still hear people on my own staff referring to them as retarded."

"I understand," said Pevnick, "but the savants—at least this group—do not see the word *savants*, in itself, as derogatory, unless it is connected with the antiquated 'idiot savant' people once used so freely. But, they know as well as I do they are certainly not idiots."

"You're doing some sort of study with them?" the President asked.

"Your people do their homework. Yes, that's right. Sir, these are some of the most remarkable people I've ever met," he said, his excitement obvious. "The world looks at them as if they're defective, or handicapped. But, I'm telling you, they're…miraculous," said Pevnick, his cheeks glowing with pride. "I was going to test their limitations in an experiment that has never been done before: a group of savants working on a common project."

"No one has ever thought of that before?"

"No. Can you believe it? They tend to be hidden in society, for the most part. If they do gain notoriety—and some of them have— they tend to work individually. By their nature, they don't know or think in terms of a team concept."

"Hmm. Well, who are they?"

As they made their way through the house, Pevnick briefed President Cooper on his unique group. "They're an international collection, for sure. James Tramwell, he's from England. He's a translator by profession, but also does *lightning calculations*. He's the one the media calls, 'Brainiac', though, understandably, he doesn't care for the term. He's the most functional of the group.

"Then, there's Harvey Peet from Australia. Remembers everything and has read tens of thousands of books. His knowledge is seemingly limitless, though he needs help doing small things like dressing himself, as do most of them, actually. The media refers to him as 'Memory Man.'"

The two men strolled through the Beehive—Cooper repeatedly glancing at his watch, as they approached the library. Pevnick continued his pre-introductions, accelerating his briefing when he noted the President's increasing anxiety. "Then, we have Jeremy Clemens, a sculptor from France with uncanny mechanical skills. He also has what is known as *perfect appreciation*, that is, he inherently knows the exact time anywhere in the world, as well as coordinates, latitude and longitude. It's like he is a human GIS gauge."

"Hmm. What do they call him?"

Pevnick chuckled. "Well, they call him 'Tool.' Not very flattering, but accurate, I'm afraid."

Cooper's now elusive smile reluctantly came back for the briefest of moments.

"Lastly, there's Etta Kim from Japan. We know the least about her, but she is able to design fantastical buildings and structures, all in three-dimension. She has an inherent knowledge of the ocean, can almost *sense* tide changes, and predicts hurricane paths with near unbelievable precision. In scientific studies, she has shown some extra sensory perception, not uncommon among savants, but remarkable if you've ever witnessed it outside a cheesy magic show. She doesn't have a nickname, at least not yet."

The two men stopped for a moment as Dr. Pevnick pondered something. The house seemed too quiet. He'd already become accustomed to the savants arguing or pestering each other. Now, there was nothing and that feeling of dread he'd experienced came back to him like a flash flood.

"As I said, I was going to have them try to work on a project together," said Pevnick hesitantly. "See how they do. How they react to group dynamics. See if their communication skills can be improved, or at least, better understood. They don't think, or solve problems like you and I do because they process information differently. It would have been interesting to see what would have come out of the collaboration. Now, with this *event*…we may never know."

They stepped into the library and found Mrs. Brown putting away stacks of books and cleaning up. It looked as if a children's daycare group had been trashing the room. The savants were not there and Pevnick's anxiety grew.

"Where are our guests, Mrs. Brown?"

She looked up, slightly frazzled, a stray strand of hair falling out of her critically pinned-up bun, her face shiny with exertion. "I'm sorry, I thought you knew. They went out to the workshop as soon as you stepped out to greet the President."

"I wonder what…" began Pevnick, feeling his heart begin to race.

Mrs. Brown was looking out the window with a quizzical look on her face. "Well, there they are now. But I wonder what in the world…?"

Through the window of the library they saw James, Harvey, Jeremy and Etta riding on a contraption: an old tractor that had undergone a quick but efficient makeover. The vehicle was covered in wire, batteries, and solar panels, bumping along the dirt road and coming from the workshop at the back of the property. As they approached in a cover of dust, Secret Service agents rushed up and surrounded the tractor. They drew their guns and one of them grabbed the driver of the vehicle—James—and pulled him out of his seat.

"Oh, my God," said Mrs. Brown, her face pressed against the glass. Dr. Pevnick and the President stood, transfixed, staring out the window.

James looked toward the window and flashed a peace sign before he was pushed face down to the ground.

"I think we better intervene," said the President.

CHAPTER SIX

Dr. Pevnick and the President rushed outside, flanked by Secret Service agents. The scene was complete chaos. Jeremy, trying to defend James, had squared off with one of the Secret Service men and three more pounced on him. He was incredibly strong and gave them a run for their money. Harvey was driving them crazy with his incessant talking and cursing; the words flowing from his mouth would shame a sailor, and he had the volume turned up all the way. Etta was stimming, her arms flailing wildly from the stress and excitement. James was calmly lying on his stomach, smiling and waiting for the agent to get off of his back. By now, the Secret Service men realized the people they are assaulting were "different" and probably no threat, but couldn't back down.

"It's okay, gentlemen," said President Cooper. "You can release them. They are guests here."

The agents released their captives and began to brush themselves off. Most of them were embarrassed, partly because they realized the savants were no threat to them, or anyone else. Partly, because trying to subdue them was more difficult than they would have thought.

Dr. Pevnick approached his group, scrutinizing the odd-looking vehicle that they rode up in. "What in the world is this?"

James methodically brushed off his trousers and re-buttoned his grass-stained shirt. "C'mon, doctor. Did you really think it would take us a month to complete this assignment?"

"Well...I...had no idea. You...all, just did this?" he asked, touching the vehicle as if to see if it was real, admiring the craftsmanship and technology that had obviously gone into it.

"It was, fu...fu...*fudge*! ...easy," said Harvey. He began to walk past one of the agents and couldn't resist. He turned and pushed the man. "Back off, bast...bass...bass...oh, hell. Turd!"

"All right, Harvey," said Pevnick. "That's enough. This was all a misunderstanding. These men were doing their job, protecting the President. Etta, are you okay?"

Etta sat on the ground holding her legs, whimpering, and rocking back and forth. Her huge eyes, wet with tears. Pevnick reached into his pocket and found another gift for her, a seashell. He handed it to her and she almost immediately stopped crying and sat very still, like a small animal hiding from a larger predator. She held the shell up to her face as if it was the only thing in the world, her fingers playing over its surface as if she was reading Braille.

"I'm sorry, Mr. President," said Pevnick. "Harvey is a *coprolalic*, that is, he involuntarily shouts curse words at times."

The President was cool. "That's all right. I do that now and then, myself. Why don't you introduce us?" He approached with his hand out, displaying the warm, winning smile that got him elected.

"Sure," said Pevnick. "This is Harvey Peet."

Harvey bowed—his favorite gesture, it seemed—sweeping his hand out in a grand arc as if he was meeting the Queen of England. "Hello, Mr. Pr...Pr...Prick, er, uh, *Pres*-ident."

Pevnick's face turned scarlet. "And, uh, this is James Tramwell."

James stepped up to President Cooper and shook his hand, then wouldn't let go. The President smiled and let James keep his hand though the Secret Service men were on high alert and moving in.

Pevnick shook his head, exasperated. "And over here is Jeremy Clemens. Uh, Jeremy, couldn't you find some pants?"

Jeremy was still wearing a sweater and underwear, his knees muddy from scuffling with the agents on the ground. "Sorry, monsieur. Sorry. My English ees not so good. My English... Eet is 11:42 in Dubai."

President Cooper extricated his limb from James and approached Jeremy, extending his hand. Jeremy just kept his arms crossed and looked at him quizzically.

Pevnick gave him a scowl and sighed. "And last, but certainly not least, this is Etta Kim," he said, helping her to her feet. She bowed in the traditional Japanese manner of respect. "Everyone, in case you don't know, this is President Cooper. He, uh, runs the United States."

Harvey continued to bow, animatedly, over and over, like a puppet out of control.

"Well, it's my pleasure," said the President. "Dr. Pevnick has told me about your project." He looked the vehicle over. "How did you finish so quickly?"

"It was easy," said James. "Harvey read all the literature we needed on the subject and told me. I translated it to Etta and she designed it. Jeremy said he could build it—he had the hardest part—he had to construct some capacitors and transducers out of copper wire and magnets, then convert this gasoline motor to electric. Once it was electric, we just needed to power it up using the sun's power. We found everything we needed in the workshop out back. Well, everything except the solar panels, which we took off the roof of Dr. Pevnick's home." James looked sheepishly at Dr. Pevnick. "Uh, sorry, doctor, we probably won't have hot water in the house tonight."

President Cooper continued to look over the vehicle with obvious admiration. "This is amazing."

"Not really," said James. "We cheated. If we wouldn't have found this old tractor, it would have taken us at least a few days to build a vehicle." Then, without missing a beat, he asked, "So, are you here to tell Dr. Pevnick about the end of the world?"

The President had been smiling broadly, until now. He glanced at Director Finney with a concerned look on his face, then back to Dr. Pevnick. "Is he clairvoyant, too?"

"No, sir. But, he can draw conclusions quickly based on mathematical probabilities."

James butted back in. "While the others worked on our solar tractor, I took the time to do some research on the web. Is the problem that unstable fault line off Cape Hatteras, or that bomb that was detonated off of Georgia the other day? Or…are the two related?"

"James, please!" said Pevnick, aggravated at his lack of respect.

The President looked stunned. Then, he noticed James was talking to him with his eyes shut. "I can't really…talk about…uh, why are you keeping your eyes closed? Is the sun bothering you?"

"No," James said, bluntly. "If I open my eyes, I'll try to count the blades of grass in this field. A weakness of mine. But, don't worry, President Cooper. We can keep a secret. We are all committed to being here for a month. As part of the project, we've been isolated from our families. None of us drive…well, obviously I can drive a tractor, but my point is, we aren't going anywhere. And if we did, who would listen to a bunch of, if you'll excuse the colloquialism, *retards*, anyway?"

"I don't care for that word, Mr. Tramwell," the President remarked.

Pevnick stepped in again, horrified at the outcome of the meeting. "I'm sorry, Mr. President. I'll address this. I know you have to be going…"

"I have a minute. Go on, James. What do you know about the situation?"

"Just what I can find on the Internet, so far. Dr. Pevnick probably told you, I do lightning calculations. I am not bragging. That is my gift and my curse. If you extend this ability to logic, which is really just a form of mathematics, it's easy to draw some conclusions."

"Go on."

"Well, I know Dr. P worked with your government previously on post-disaster probabilities before and after Katrina. Suddenly, you show up at his research facility. I deduced you were not coming for a social call."

"And from that you were able to get to an impending disaster?"

"Well, not quite. I have an online business; I work with communications and am a consultant to various international corporations and interests, primarily doing translations and so forth. I am on the Internet constantly. There is so much information out there that it almost overwhelms me, but if I focus, I can put things together."

James squinted through his eyelids and approached the President, his arm extended. The Secret Service men grew edgy, but President Cooper held up his hand to let them know it was okay. James reached the President and looked into his face, inches away as a deliberate distraction from the grass he was compelled to count. He continued his explanation, speaking quickly and mechanically.

"A few days ago, when Etta and I first met, she told me she had a feeling there was something wrong with the ocean. I was not alarmed, initially, but the more I came to know her, the more I realized how outstanding her abilities are. I began doing some searches on the web. I drew some conclusions. I looked for disasters around the world that might affect the oceans. No significant storms anywhere. No giant oil spills. But there was a tabloid report of a possible nuclear detonation off the eastern coast yesterday. It was confirmed by an old, outdated nuclear monitoring project called Vela. There is a small group of people, sort of like ham radio operators, who still monitor the project, though it almost never shows anything. It's like those people who are always monitoring the skies, looking for alien life, you know? Did you know Vela means *vigil* in Spanish? Anyway, I found some old stories about a bomb that went missing some fifty years ago. Then, while exploring that subject, I found some articles about the continental shelf off Cape Haterras. It's much farther away than where the bomb was presumed to have been lost, but this was a particularly powerful bomb, wasn't it, Mr. President?"

The President didn't answer, but he felt an icy sweat form on the back of his neck as he wondered: *who else can put this together if this young man can?*

"Anyway," James continued, "there are entire websites devoted to the subject of various potential tsunamis striking the U.S. due to tectonic plate shifts and so forth. But, the one that poses the most danger is the Cape Haterras fault. Most believe that when the fault fails, it will cause a massive underwater landslide that will, in turn, cause a massive tidal wave. This wave is believed to be what will trigger an Armageddon, if you will, in the United States. I haven't done so yet, but I could make calculations on the economic collapse..."

President Cooper interrupted him, "So, when I came here today, you drew the conclusion that I came to ask Dr. Pevnick for his advice again?"

"Of course. And, it isn't hurricane season yet."

"I see." The President pondered the information. As he did, a flock of birds flew overhead, in formation again, and he watched them as if he were looking to nature for some answers. The answer he found only added to his anxiety. A great deal of wildlife would be lost, too. Something most people didn't consider when they study disasters. Zoos and wildlife collections are not part of a National Emergency Plan. He regretted this massive oversight, but knew he had to focus on the people and the infrastructures for now. He swallowed dryly and took the needed time to compose himself.

"Well," Cooper said, "it has been…interesting to meet you all. I…wish you luck. Stephen, we'll talk tomorrow."

"Yes, sir. Thank you…for your patience."

"Is that it?" asked James, perturbed. "Are you done talking with me, Mr. President?"

President Cooper, walking toward his car, stopped and looked back. "I'm afraid so. Even if you're right, James, I could not discuss it with you. It would be a matter of national security."

James smiled. "You just told me everything I need to know, sir, except for one thing."

"And that is?"

"If such a scenario did happen, is there a plan for it?"

The President's face grew grim. "How could anyone plan for something like that?"

"I don't know," said James sarcastically. "I lead a sheltered life. But, have any of your people in the scientific community, or your military come up with a contingency plan?"

"James," said Pevnick, "please don't be disrespectful!"

The President continued toward his waiting car. "I'm sorry, but I have to go. You're a brilliant young man, James. I hope we meet again someday."

"Sure. I'll just tread water until then," he said with passion, if not outright anger, in his voice. "Before you leave, listen to this and ask your scientists—you know, the ones that are not *disabled* like me? Ask them this simple question: could they not reduce the inertia energy by reducing the force?"

President Cooper turned back to James. "What do you mean by that?"

"Remove as much of the deteriorating shelf before it fails, and you will lessen its impact."

"Really?" said the President. It was difficult to say if he was being sarcastic—that was not his way—but his tone had taken on an edginess as his patience wore thin.

"Yes," said James, confidently. "My calculations suggest for every one hundred billion tons of earth moved, we would reduce the kinetic energy by one thousand trillion joules. Depending on how it was moved, that much might save, oh…New York, or maybe Florida, and it would certainly reduce the impact on America overall."

There was a tense moment as the President contemplated James's theory, his jaw muscles working. Jeremy broke the tension as he approached the President with a gift: a small figurine of Abraham Lincoln that he had fashioned out of copper wire. He handed it to President Cooper.

"Copper for Cooper! Copper for Cooper! Zee time in New Delhi is 12:44, in zee morning."

President Cooper's smile returned as he accepted the gift, cautiously keeping an eye on Jeremy, who moved away, walking backward, smiling from ear to ear. The President's car pulled up behind him. The door was opened for him and he got in, placing the copper figure in his shirt pocket. As the car pulled away, the President stared out the window at James. The young man was doing something with his hands, gesturing at him. As a father of a deaf child, he had learned to read and utilize some sign language. He recognized James was signing to him. He squinted back at him through the tinted window, trying to remember the meanings of the hand motions and realized as they pulled away what James was saying: *Tell your daughter everything will be okay.* President Cooper felt a chill run down his back; goose bumps formed on his flesh.

CHAPTER SEVEN

Etta Kim: Acquired Savant

Eight years ago: Shizouka, Japan

Etta watched her sister's friends running around the pool, jumping in, splashing water, while the mothers flitted around the patio table, setting up birthday balloons, laying out paper plates and cupcakes. It was busy and loud.

Her sister was turning seven, and so they were doing the Shichi-go-san Festival, or Seven-Five-Three Festival, a very special day for Japanese children. Etta had learned that these ages were celebrated at one time because children often did not live past those ages, though most people had forgotten that eerie origin. She was nine then, and past that age, but she remembered her Shichi-go-san as a party that lasted all day and into the evening, and she received so many gifts, including some nice, tinted swimming goggles that she still used in their pool.

Their family was very well-to-do. Her father was a scientist who worked at the nearby nuclear power plant in Shizouka and made a lot of money. Her mother had obtained a doctoral degree in ocean sciences in the United States and taught at the university until Etta's sister was born, then became a stay at home mother. They often went on beach vacations where they snorkeled together and, very early on, Etta learned to love the sea. Their home was close enough to it for her to smell the ocean. With a view of the mountains from their backyard, they felt like they lived in heaven, save the occasional rumble of the earthquakes that were common to the area.

The smaller girls were splashing Etta so much, she decided she might as well just jump in again, and take the pool back over. "I'm a sea serpent," she exclaimed, spreading her fingers and arms wide in an attempt to make herself look fierce. All the little girls screamed. As she splashed in, a roar of giggles went up and the smaller girls got out of the pool to continue their melee, which included an assault on the sea serpent with blow-up beach balls. Etta laughed and dove down where the silence of the water around her was comforting. She could hold her breath for a long time, and she cruised along the pool bottom like a flounder.

Above the water, the girls started to beg for the waterslide to be turned on so they could launch themselves at the "serpent." One of the children's fathers heard their pleas, strolled over to the pool pump, and pushed the lever for the waterfall to the "On" position.

In that particular pump configuration, when the waterfall was turned on, it shifted the suction of the pool's skimmer to the bottom drain to feed the flow of the waterfall with an abundance of water. Recently, Etta's father had noted the vented cover for that suction was broken. He'd removed the cover and had meant to replace it with a new one before the party, but got busy with his work and forgot to do it.

Etta was still inching along the bottom of the pool, feeling the tug of her lungs wanting fresh air, and preparing to pop up and scare the other kids with her rendition of a kraken popping out of the sea. She was hovering an inch over the suction port when the waterfall was turned on and it pulled her down with a force as strong as a crocodile's bite. She tried not to panic as the soft skin of her abdomen was sucked into the hole so strongly that it felt like the flesh would rip, and it caused her to lose some of her breath. She placed her hands against the pool bottom, and tried to push herself up, but she wasn't strong enough. The exertion of trying to pull away caused her to run out of breath.

Above, the surface of the pool was covered with floating toys and rafts, the water churned by the downpour of the waterfall and the dozen kids foaming up the water so much it appeared to be filled with feeding piranha. The bottom of the pool was obscured, as was the struggle Etta was enduring.

As the last of the life-giving air left her lungs, Etta realized, and oddly accepted, she was going to drown. She fought to keep the water from entering her mouth initially, but her hungry lungs won the fight, and as she weakened, her mouth went slack and the water rushed in. There was the inevitable laryngospasm that closed off her airway, so very little water made it into her lungs. But, without oxygen, her consciousness began to fade and with it, the pain of drowning eased. Though her eyes were still open, the vision began to darken as if she were looking up from a black velvet bag as someone drew its strings closed.

The earthquake was not a big one by Japanese standards; a four on their Shindo scale. But it shook the Kim's home enough to topple the patio cake and spill the treats and goodie bags. Children stumbled about and fell, and some scraped their knees as their parents tried to come to their rescue. The rock waterfall trembled, and the pipes that fed it water burst. Then it was over, and the quiet that followed the quake was almost as eerie as the tremors.

"Everyone okay?" someone yelled. Some of the children were crying, but a few of them were delighted.

"That was so cool!" exclaimed one of the kids.

Etta's father looked about hurriedly. He saw his youngest daughter right away; she ran up and gave him a hug with tears in her eyes. But he did not see Etta. He began to panic. "Has anyone seen Etta?" he called out, just as her body floated to the surface of the pool.

"Oh, no," he screamed, as he jumped into the pool.

Etta's mother saw what happened and, without hesitating, called in the emergency and requested an ambulance. By the time she got off the phone, Mr. Kim had Etta laid out on the patio, a few of the other parents gathered around her trying to offer help.

Mrs. Kim had learned CPR while living in the United States. As she approached her daughter's lifeless body, the lessons she'd learned so long ago came back to her. She knelt next to Etta, noted her eyes were open, the pupils fixed and dilated, her lips blue. Feeling her neck, she detected no pulse. She put her face next to Etta's mouth, but no breath brushed her cheek. She opened Etta's mouth, placed her own over it, and blew air into her lungs. She did this twice before sliding her hands along her daughter's rib cage and locating the arch just below her heart. Mrs. Kim placed her hands on the lower part of Etta's sternum and began pushing on her chest. She continued doing the compressions, while Mr. Kim took over blowing into Etta's mouth. One of the guests found a beach towel and covered Etta's legs in an attempt to keep her warm.

By the time the ambulance arrived, Mr. and Mrs. Kim had managed to get a pulse back in Etta and she had taken a few gasping breaths. But she had not regained consciousness, and would not for several days.

Etta was taken to a very good hospital where her vital signs— heart rate, breathing, temperature, blood pressure—all became normal again, but the doctors told the Kims her brain had been too long without oxygen. If she regained consciousness, she would not be the same. What exactly did that mean? The doctors could not be sure. Time would tell.

When she did regain consciousness, Etta did not recognize anything or anyone around her. Once a brilliant student, she could not remember how to speak or even walk.

She had months of extensive physical therapy and eventually learned to walk again, but her growth was altered, she would always remain somewhat small. Her mental state was questionable. Talking came in muted grunts and squeaks. She would scream at times and have what was at first thought to be seizures, her arms flailing about. Later the doctors called it "stimming," and said it was from her brain being denied oxygen for so long.

Her parents hired trained medical professionals to come to the house and watch over her, help her to be "normal" again. Usually, Etta was quiet, but at times she was quite trying, grunting and stimming and marking up the furniture and walls with whatever she could find. One of the nurses finally, as a last resort, thought she knew what would make her happy; she gave her some drawing paper and colored pencils to settle her down.

Within a few hours, working in complete silence, Etta drew some machines. They were not just fantastical machines either. When her father came home from the nuclear plant that day, he looked over her drawings. He'd seen something like them at the plant; they seemed to be part of a turbine-driven water cooling system they used for cooling the nuclear reactors. But, the ones his daughter had drawn seemed different—improved, perhaps. He took some to work the next day, and showed them to one of the engineers he considered a friend. The engineer, Mr. Sato, was amazed. He asked if Mr. Kim had shown his daughter some of the plant's engineering and reminded him that some of the internal workings in the plant were confidential. Mr. Kim assured him he had not.

That evening, Mr. Sato accompanied Mr. Kim home to meet Etta. During that day, Etta had filled her sketch pad with a variety of machines so advanced, Mr. Sato was without words. He tried to talk to her with Mr. Kim attempting to translate as Etta could only grunt answers to the engineer's questions.

As they talked, though, Etta suddenly stopped, her eyes going wide, looking at a wall behind them, as if she could see something they could not. Her face turned red with the effort, but she spoke the first full, recognizable words since her accident.

"Tec…tectonic plates are shifting," she stuttered. "The…ocean… is upset. There's going to be an earthquake in…soon."

Mr. and Mrs. Kim and Mr. Sato all looked at each other, mouths hanging open. Mrs. Kim covered her mouth with her hands as tears began to stream down her face. Mr. Kim talked to their daughter first.

"What…do you mean, Etta?" he asked. "How…would you know that?"

Etta looked at him as if he were blind. "I can…see it. You should go," she said, mechanically. "You…have…time. It won't hit…for another hour. Go *now*. Go to that plant and…make it safe."

"But…," Mr. Kim began.

Etta grew alarmed. To her it was like the house was on fire and no one else could see the flames but her. "Go now," she said, raising her voice. "*Go now.*"

Mr. Kim looked at Mr. Sato, and said, "Maybe we should go?"

Mr. Sato nodded, looking at Etta's drawings. "Okay," he said, thoughtfully. "It couldn't hurt. We could check to make sure the back-up coolers will turn on if there is a power failure. We're supposed to do that monthly for a drill, but I've been so busy the past few months, I haven't had time."

Etta stood up and came over to the man. She took his hand in hers and began to squeeze it, so hard he had to pull it away.

"*Please,*" she said, urgently. "Go now."

It was an unsettling moment and the men stood up hesitantly. "I'd…like to come back some time and talk to you about your drawings," said the engineer.

Etta nodded, then said again, more urgently, "Go now."

Mr. Kim and the engineer drove back to the plant in conversation, trying to figure out what Etta was going on about, when the first siren in the earthquake warning system sounded.

They finished checking the back-up cooling system when they felt the first tremors. An alarm went off and a recording began telling all personnel to evacuate the building. As Mr. Kim began making his way through the crowd in the parking lot, he looked toward the sea and saw the tide going out so quickly that fish were being left in the sand, flopping about. Having lived through a tsunami when he was a child, he knew what that meant. It was time to go.

They quickly checked the back-up coolers, and found a start-up glitch that was easily traced to a circuit that had been inadvertently left in the "Off" position. It was turned back on, and the men, assured the units were functioning, then raced back to the car. Mr. Kim sped uphill toward the mountaintop and the safety of their home, just as the tsunami began to push into the shoreline.

In the aftermath, thousands of people were displaced when their homes were washed away in the lowlands, and many lives were lost. The nuclear power facility where Mr. Kim worked was mostly destroyed and, though the initial generator coolers did fail, the back-up coolers sustained their function, keeping the nuclear generators stable, and greatly reduced the devastation that could have resulted if the plant had failed.

Mr. Sato mentioned the incident with Etta Kim to a friend who worked with the media. Within a couple of weeks, after some stability was returned to the area and the community was beginning to recover, the Kim's house was inundated with local journalists, initially, but soon reporters from countries as far away as the United

Kingdom and the United States began to show up to meet the girl who could predict tsunamis. Within a few months, Etta Kim was talking better, though she still exhibited some distressful signs of her accident, such as physical tics and broken speech patterns. But she began to write research papers and design machines for engineering industry magazines and businesses. She wrote books and appeared on television shows, though her appearances were often uncomfortable interviews throughout which few people could understand what she was trying to explain.

CHAPTER EIGHT

Washington, D.C.: Present

The man stepped out of his black town car and walked hurriedly across the spongy grass of the oddly vacant Mall, pulling a satellite phone out of his trench coat. He walked along in the shadows of the tree line, while two Secret Service men flanked him at an ordered distance. With his yellow-tinted shooting glasses and wool fedora—a fashion piece he was pleased to see return to style—he was not recognizable. When the phone vibrated, he put it to his ear and talked in whispers.

"Go ahead. Yes, this is an encrypted phone. Can't be bugged. We can talk. Yes, the President is doing exactly what we thought he'd do. I can say with confidence, Operation Ragnarok begins now. Once our military is in place, we can proceed with the plan. Like we discussed, it doesn't matter what he decides to do, it's a no-win outcome for him. If he evacuates, we go to martial law. If he doesn't evacuate, we give it to the press, people self-evacuate, and we go to martial law. Yes, we have to with that many people moving. No, the National Guard is not going to be a problem, bunch of weekend warriors that'll wet their pants and run for the hills the first shot we fire over their heads. It's time we take back our country, General. You just make sure the militias are ready and take care of those loose ends we identified. If someone figures out we moved that device onto the fault line…well, just make sure no one does."

***

Alexandria, Virginia

Guy McAllister, late sixties, prepared to leave his house. He was one of those guys who always forgets things, so he would get to the door, place his hand on the knob, then turn and look back into the living room, as if it would somehow tell him what he was forgetting. As a former CIA agent and nautical specialist, he had accumulated many things over the years serving his country. There was a plaque on the wall commemorating his 25 years of distinguished service and a picture of him with the President, shaking hands. Another picture of him in his naval uniform, standing in front of a giant submarine that looked like a whale surfacing behind him. There were pictures of his children and their children.

He saw what he was looking for—his car keys—and went back to fetch them off the roll top desk where he did his bills and correspondence. Back to the door, hand on knob, glance back at the room, check pockets. Yes, wallet was there, cell phone, and now keys. Ready to go.

McAllister strolled out to his car, unlocking it with the remote before getting to it. Once in the car, he looked in the rearview mirror and primped his hair. Checked his smile to see if any breakfast lingered in his teeth. Clean and shiny. Satisfied he was ready to go, he pushed the key into the ignition and started the car.

There was a blinding flash and the car erupted into a fire ball that sent pieces of the car onto roofs of nearby houses and set fire to the American flag that stood in front of McAllister's home.

***

Cape Cod, Massachusetts

Former Naval Commander Anthony Johnson was sitting on the wrap-around veranda of his clapboard home near the ocean. He looked like a model from an L.L.Bean catalogue. Handsome face, with just enough weathered lines to give him character. Thick silver streaked hair, combed back stylishly. A large barrel chest balanced over a still trim waist; not bad for a retired, lifelong seaman. He sipped a cup of steaming coffee and watched as a postal carrier approached his house. Funny, it was a little early in the day for mail.

The postman was built like an engine block, short and wide. He stopped, looked to both sides and even turned before approaching the veranda. He was carrying a package tightly under one arm. He walked up the steps mechanically. "Mr. Anthony Johnson?" he inquired.

"Yes?" said Johnson.

"Admiral Johnson?" asked the postman.

"Well, yes. But no one has called me that in a long time…"

The postman pulled his hand from under the package and extended it toward Johnson. It was holding a gun with a long silencer tip attached. The gun went, "*Thwit, thwit.*"

Johnson dropped his coffee, the ceramic mug shattering as it hit the ground. The former admiral stood, groaned once then fell to the ground, dead.

The postman turned and walked quickly away.

***

A bar in North Harbor, Maine

A group of sailors—burly, unshaven, wearing Navy pea coats—were huddled around the beer-soaked, worn bar. They drank frothy lagers as they waited on their fried fish and chips and told preposterous stories of living on the sea. It was quiet in the bar, other than the rowdy seamen who were all regulars there. It was a Monday, a slow day for business, so the singular waitress who usually worked there was given the day off. The tired bartender wearily dried glasses with a bar rag as he listened to the men's tales of travel, women who broke their hearts, and exotic ports of call where other women eagerly waited for them. He'd heard all the stories before.

The entry door to the bar slammed open with a shuttering bang. Two men entered, standing stiffly, wearing mirrored sunglasses, their hair in crew cuts. They were dressed in Army fatigues under long trench coats from which they quickly produced semiautomatic weapons.

The bartender was aghast, but managed to utter these last words: "Now, that's something you don't see every day."

The sailors turned to have a look just as the soldiers raised their rifles and opened fire. Several of the men were cut down immediately, but a couple dove over the bar to join the bartender hiding there. One of the soldiers ran over to the bar, looked behind it, and opened fire, hitting everyone who'd attempted to take cover. The soldiers rejoined at the door and looked around before exiting. The bar was quiet again, gun smoke hung in the air like thick fog off the sea. The two soldiers hid the guns under their long coats and quickly walked out into the cool afternoon.

One of the sailors lying on the ground moaned and coughed, blood flecked his lips. His trembling hand made its way down to his coat pocket and pulled out a cell phone. With one bloody finger, he managed to dial 9-1-1, and croaked, "Help. We need help. We've been…shot." Then, he dropped the phone and lost consciousness.

CHAPTER NINE

Dr. Pevnick and his "test subjects" were back in the library. Pevnick paced the room angrily, his hands alternately pushing through his hair, as if this action might somehow soothe him. It wasn't working. His jaw muscles were clenched, and there was a vein sticking out on his forehead that the group had not noticed before.

"You needn't have been so disrespectful, James," said Pevnick. "I consider the President a friend of mine…not to mention, the leader of the free world!"

"Time, or the lack of it, dictates that I have to be blunt," said James, his voice without inflection. Then, he added wryly, "Besides, don't you know savants struggle with social skills?"

"Now you're just being flippant," said Pevnick.

James looked down at his feet, taking the scolding and resisting the urge to bend down and re-tie his shoes. "I'm sorry," he whispered.

Dr. Pevnick went back to pacing the room. He wasn't ready for James to apologize so quickly. He wished he would say some other smart aleck thing so he could really lay into him, but he was losing his steam. His professional composure was coming back.

Jeremy jumped in, holding up Pevnick's watch. "Your watch, monsieur. Watch. Watch. Zee time, eet ees per-fect! Now, better zen new." He paused before adding, "In Edinburgh, eet ees 10:38. Also, I have put my pants on. *Oui*? Pants on."

That made Pevnick smile. He accepted the watch, and put it back on his wrist.

"Obviously, our project is going to have to be put on hold, indefinitely. I've got a lot of work to do. Please, all of you, make yourselves comfortable. I'll…have Mrs. Brown work on getting you all back home, safely. We'll, uh, talk more tomorrow. Just… make yourselves at home until then. I, uh, I'm sorry. None of us were expecting this…crisis. Please excuse me."

James held up a hand. "Excuse me, Dr. Pevnick, but when do you think you will have your report ready?"

Pevnick looked confused. "I'm going to try to have something ready by tomorrow afternoon."

James looked around at his colleagues as if to silently recruit them into the conversation. He held out both hands, palms up. "Why don't you let us help? Surely Harvey could provide some demographic information. He knows the population of every city in the United States."

Harvey looked up from a book he'd just finished reading in the time it takes most people to make some breakfast. "As well as the zip codes and directions to any, damn, damn, damn, address."

Dr. Pevnick was about to dismiss the idea, but something made him hesitate. This was not business as usual. This was a disaster; one of such gravity, most people had never experienced anything like it. He pondered the proposal. *At least it would keep them busy,* he thought to himself. Besides, they were good researchers. *Can't hurt, might help,* he thought. "Actually, James, that's not a bad idea. In fact, it might be quite useful. You're on."

"On what?" asked Jeremy, perplexed.

Pevnick looked at him and smiled. "It's just an expression, Jeremy. It means I'll accept James's offer. Yes, I could use your help."

"Oh, okay! Zen I am in."

"Great," said James. "I'll get started on how we can stop the disaster…" He opened a laptop he had tucked under his arm and began typing immediately, as if he could easily find a site on how to save the world.

Pevnick looked at him quizzically. "Eh, what?"

James continued to type.

"Look, James, I appreciate your…willingness to try to help, but from what the President said, there is nothing that can be done. If there were, I'm sure they would be doing it."

James glanced up. "Oh? Just like when they knew the Nazis were launching a war on Europe and they did nothing until the war came to the U.S. via Pearl Harbor?" He returned to typing.

"That's different," said Pevnick. "A different time..."

"Uh-huh," said James. "And what about Hurricane Katrina? You worked on a plan with this same government a year before that storm and they ignored your suggestions. Hundreds could have been saved...."

"That's enough, James," said Pevnick, the heat of his anger rising again. "I don't have time to debate this with you."

"I've already been thinking of some plans, Dr. Pevnick. Actually, several plans they could try."

Pevnick held up his hand. "If you want to spend the next day or two researching some science fiction scheme, you go ahead. I have *real* work to do." He pushed abruptly past the others and out of the room, shaking his head as he went.

***

Washington, D.C. The Oval Office

It was after ten o'clock at night, but President Cooper had summoned Dr. Hisamoto and Dr. Heimel to the White House for a private discussion. They were all obviously fatigued, but Cooper seemed to possess boundless energy; whiskered chin, loosened tie, and all. His staff brought a shining urn of steaming coffee into the room as the three men huddled around the President's gargantuan desk. It appeared it was going to be a long night.

"I'm sorry to pull you two in here so late, but I know you realize the gravity of this situation."

"Of course, Mr. President," said Heimel.

"You gentlemen seem to be the most informed of this situation," said Cooper, "so I'm going to go out on a limb here. Answer something for me, and if you don't know, go ahead and make your best guess. Okay?"

"Yes, sir?" said Hisamoto, leaning forward with interest.

"If we could remove some of the deteriorating ocean shelf, could that possibly reduce the impact of the event?"

Both of the scientists looked at each other then slowly, wordlessly, nodded.

"The problem is," said Heimel, "is that the wall is approximately six-hundred-feet deep and dozens of miles long. What kind of equipment could move that much land mass, and at that depth?"

Hisamoto interjected, "It would be a suicide mission. Anyone in the vicinity of that shelf when it fails would perish."

"I understand," said Cooper, "but, throughout history, we have always found brave men willing to make sacrifices for their countries. I believe we still can. As for the equipment? I'll leave that up to the Army Corps of Engineers. Maybe they can come up with something." The President sat up and leaned forward in his chair. "I'm going to mobilize them immediately."

Hisamoto blinked rapidly and cleared his throat. "I…suppose it would be better than doing nothing at all."

"Agreed," said Heimel. "But, the more people assigned to the mitigation, the more likely the media will find out."

"Maybe not," said Cooper. "Like you said, the problem is six-hundred-feet deep. They can't get camera crews down there easily, if at all. And if they do find out, at least they'll know that we are trying to do *something*. That might give the nation hope. I think that's the best thing we can offer right now." He got up and poured himself some coffee, then turned back to the two scientists. "I'm going to begin evacuation in forty-eight hours. If we can make a dent in this thing, maybe I won't have to evacuate as many areas. The more we can contain it, the better off we all are. I'm going to ask you men to work with the Department of Defense's top engineers. Put your thinking caps on, gentlemen. Let's try to generate some hope."

Heimel stood, nodded, and shook the President's hand. Hisamoto stood, and bowed slightly. Cooper returned the gesture.

Hisamoto turned back to the President as he was going out the door of his office. He cleared his throat, and said, "Try to get some rest when you can, Mr. President."

Cooper nodded and smiled benignly. "You, too."

CHAPTER TEN

The moon shone over a secluded part of a forest in northeastern Pennsylvania. From the air, it appeared to be nothing more than a forest canopy, but underneath the thick foliage, military vehicles moved men and equipment through a maze of camouflaged bunkers and tents. The scent of pine in the air was pervasive, mixed with the fumes of smoke. Generators thrummed and provided lighting to the people who were working here, *preparing* there.

In one of the bunkers, Vice President Proger was meeting with General Aristotle Haufman. The General was in his fifties; an ash colored crew cut sat atop his head that appeared to be made from steel shavings. His face was stern, determined, with an edge of bitterness from having compromised his own ideals for so long. His opinions had "upset" some of his peers over the years. For example, his willingness to launch bold infantry attacks when covert operations might have served the Army's mission better wasn't popular, neither was his willingness to utilize torture tactics that were banned worldwide. These things had been discussed in closed rooms, in hushed whispers, and had prevented him from becoming one of the "chosen few" who shared confidences and strategies with the President's circle. Still, his men respected him—or feared him—and he commanded total obedience from them.

"Are the men ready, General?" said Proger, shaking the general's hand.

"Yes, sir. We are armed, ready, and motivated in every state, including those west of the 'event' area. We've begun to pull our militias out of the eastern seaboard, moving them several hundreds of miles inland. In all, we have some half-million troops at the ready, sir."

"Excellent," said Proger. The President has said we'll keep forces fifty miles inland, but from everything I've heard, that may be too close. They'll probably lose half the available Army as soon as it happens."

"And the rest will be so dumbstruck," Haufman added, "they'll disband and fall apart. I wouldn't be surprised if some of them came to us as the new military and joined us. There will be soldiers looking for leadership and purpose, especially after the widespread devastation.

Proger nodded in agreement. "And the other matter; you took care of the, uh, other considerations?"

"Of course, sir. The crew of the sub have all been eliminated. It's part of the mission, sir."

"Yes. Good. I don't need to tell you what would happen if it leaked out that we moved a bomb out there." He paused to consider something and shook his head. "Hell, we were only moving the bomb out there to minimize the fall out on shore."

"Of course, sir. How could we know there was a fault line there?"

Proger rubbed his jaw, thinking. "Look, I know our plan changed. We didn't anticipate the tidal wave they're now predicting will engulf the entire east coast, but…"

"But, it's better this way," said Haufman, enthusiastically. His eyes gleamed, fueled by a vision he'd harbored for years. "The President will have most of the armed forces in the hot zone. The troop casualties will be catastrophic, God rest their souls. Our militia will move in and enforce martial law on the fringes of the devastation area. Civilians will be scared, their spirits broken. They'll be easily maneuvered, like cattle. The President can't risk air strikes or bombing without incurring massive civilian casualties. So, it'll have to be a guerilla war and we already know the U.S. Military isn't very accomplished in that area. The President will appear impotent and useless. The nation will be looking for new leadership and direction."

Vice President Proger grinned. "That's where I'll come in," he said, "just as we've planned. Instead of showing Cooper as just a weak leader who could allow a nuclear bomb to be detonated right off the nation's coast, we'll show him as an indecisive president in times of a true crisis. History has shown conquered nations quickly adhere to their new leadership. It won't take long for the nation to embrace our militias. We'll build a better America. Then, we'll show the world what we're really made of."

"I'm looking forward to a new dawn, sir."

"*New dawn.* I like that. Let's rename this strike. Keep your men vigil, General. Operation 'New Dawn' begins as soon as the tide subsides."

Haufman maneuvered behind the desk in his makeshift office and opened a drawer. He withdrew a bottle of good whiskey and filled two glasses with the brown liquid.

"To you, Mr. President," said Haufman.

The two men toasted and downed their drinks in one huge, satisfying gulp.

CHAPTER ELEVEN

The sun came up over the ocean the next day, peaked into the windows of the Beehive, and found Dr. Pevnick seated at his desk, his eyes red and tired. He sipped some coffee, studied his computer screen for a few moments, and continued typing.

Harvey Peet entered the office looking as if he just woke up, unshaven, hair mussed, glasses smudged and crooked, wearing a wrinkled shirt and underwear that did not appear to have been changed for perhaps several days. He squinted like a bat at the light in the room. "The sh…*cuss, cuss,* sun is up."

Pevnick looked up at him. "Harvey, would it be too much for me to ask you to take a bath today?"

Harvey shrugged. "You can ask." He reached over and stuck his finger in Pevnick's coffee. "That's disgusting. Cold coffee. Indeed!" He wandered around the office as if he were lost, pulling a book off the shelf and reading—almost finishing it—within a few minutes. "Will there be anything else, Dr. Pevnick?"

"Huh?" he said, distracted. "Er, uh, no, Harvey. God, you've been great. I could never have finished this report so quickly without you. You're amazing!"

Harvey grinned and wiped his glasses with the tail of his shirt that was tucked into his underwear. "That's what all the women tell me."

Pevnick smiled for the first time since he and the President talked the day before. "Why don't you get some rest? Your parents would be furious with me if they knew I'd kept you up all night."

"Yeah," said Harvey, rolling his eyes. "Then you wouldn't get any fu...fu...frikkin' ice cream." He picked up the book again and raced through the pages, then stopped abruptly and slammed it shut. "Thanks for letting me help, Dr. Pevnick. This is the first time I've felt like an adult."

Pevnick wasn't sure what to say to that, but pondered what it meant.

"When you are *afflicted*, as we are," Harvey said, "people assume you are dumb."

"People...are..." Pevnick struggled with what to say.

"S'okay, Dr. Pevnick. You cannot possibly find the right words for those people, such as we know them."

Pevnick nodded in agreement. "Are the others still asleep?"

Harvey shrugged. "Jeremy, the bastich, *cuss, cuss*, might be. But James and Etta were up all night, too."

"Really?"

"Yeah. I think he—James, that is—might be sweet on Miss Etta. Ha, ha! You should see what they've been doing."

"I'm almost afraid to ask."

"You better go see for yourself. I'm going to, fu...*cuss, cuss*, sleep."

Pevnick stood up, his knees popping, and rubbed his tired eyes as Harvey stumbled off to bed. He ambled through the facility feeling that loss one endures after pulling away from an all-nighter on the computer. Mrs. Brown had made some fresh coffee, and Pevnick found his way to the aroma and poured himself another cup.

He found James and Etta sleeping in the study with their heads on the conference table, a small puddle of drool escaping Etta's mouth. Taped to the bookshelves were elaborate pencil drawings, picture after picture of fantastical mechanisms the likes of which few people had ever seen or imagined. On the computer, images of downloads popped onto the screen, one after the other. Pevnick watched the screen flash from one diagram to the next, observing the similarities of mechanized devices: explosive and nuclear devices, torpedoes, and blueprints of satellites. He yawned, shook his head, and patted Etta on the head, then slipped out of the room quiet as a cat, glancing back once more at the slumbering couple and closing the door behind him.

He sauntered down the hall, jotting notes on his stenographer's tablet. He came to a door of the bedroom farthest removed from the rest of the living quarters. His hand rested on the door knob for a moment before turning it. Mrs. Brown and a nurse assistant, a thick, strong Haitian woman in her forties named Magritte, were just finishing placing a young man into a wheelchair. He was Douglas Pevnick, Stephen's seventeen-year-old son, whom most people believed to be dead. They fussed over cleaning him up and tucking a blanket in around him. His limbs were thin and angled, like crooked branches on a tree, due to muscular atrophy. He made humming noises and grunts; spittle on his lips, one of his hands was in constant motion, as if he held an invisible pencil in his fingers and was trying to scribe a note.

Mrs. Brown glanced at Dr. Pevnick, a flash of heated emotion in her eyes as she wheeled Douglas over to the window and opened the drapes, allowing sunlight to fill the room like melted butter.

"Good morning, doctor," said Mrs. Brown.

"Good morning, Mrs. Brown," replied Pevnick, aware of the woman's disdain; she didn't approve of the doctor's regard for his own son. "Is he all right this morning?"

"Well, *Douglas*, seems particularly agitated. Somehow, he got hold of a pen left next to his bed and made a bunch of marks on his sheets. When we stripped the bed so we could wash the sheets, he became very upset. I think he wants to look outside. In fact, I think he wants to *go* outside...." She reached down and combed the young man's hair with her fingers.

"We've discussed this before, Mrs. Brown. His brain is half gone from the accident. Douglas can't tell if he is inside or outside, and—"

"I know what *you* think," said Mrs. Brown, indignant. "But, if you ask me, even a mole likes to peek its head out now and then. What could it hurt?"

"When we tried it before he had seizures from the light, went into a coma, and woke up with pneumonia that almost killed him."

"Well, if you ask me..."

"What?" said Pevnick, his turn to be annoyed.

"I...I'm sorry, doctor. We all had a late night."

Pevnick gathered himself. "It's okay. I'll sit with him for a while before I take a nap. Maybe I'll just lay down here in his bed. I'll call if I need you."

"As you wish, sir."

"Thank you. And thank you, Magritte."

Magritte nodded, her eyes glancing back and forth between Mrs. Brown and the doctor. Mrs. Brown was aware of the friction that existed between the two, but did her best to stay out of it.

Pevnick went to his son's side and brushed his hair back, then leaned over and kissed his head. He inadvertently left the writing tablet and pen on the windowsill in front of Douglas. There were scars on his son's forehead that extended down the side of his face and around his head, like a jigsaw puzzle. The young man stared up into the sky and did not respond to his father's touch, but his hand began to move again in its jerky, telegraphic fashion. Tears welled in Pevnick's eyes and fell to the blanket that covered Douglas. He turned away so Douglas wouldn't see him. Lying on the bed, he watched his son staring out the window, like a statue.

"I wish your mother was still here," said Pevnick, letting his tears soak into the pillow, fatigue pulling at him until he finally fell asleep.

Douglas's hand skittered from under the blanket and found the damp spot from his father's tear. The hand's spasmodic movement stopped as the young man felt the wetness. His eyes closed for a moment, then opened again to gaze out the window and linger on a movement he saw in the trees. The branches were filled with birds. At once, they all leapt into the sky, regrouped into a formation, moving one way, then the other, but never leaving the sight of the young man in the wheelchair. Suddenly, Douglas's hand shot up unsteadily and grabbed the writing tablet on the windowsill, though the effort exhausted him as if he'd just run a marathon.

CHAPTER TWELVE

The sun turned the White House orange as it rose in the east. It was as if this was just another day of waking up in a bright and hopeful world. But it wasn't. Inside, the President was in the Oval Office, reclining on a couch in front of a table cluttered with papers and Post-it stickers. He was asleep until the phone rang and roused him. He bolted up, fully awake, but disoriented.

"Good morning, Mr. President," said Proger.

Cooper cleared his throat. "Morning, Stan. How are you? Get any rest?"

"Yes, sir. Fully rested. Ready to get started."

"On?"

"We've got a press conference set up in thirty minutes."

"What? Who ordered that?"

"Uh, I did, sir. The press secretary has been barraged by phone calls all night, from all over the world. I've received calls from most of the big networks: NBC, CNN and, of course, Fox. Someone even put Matt Lauer through to me."

"What are you telling me, Stan?"

"I had to stall them. I told them you would do a public address this morning to answer any concerns or rumors."

"But, I wanted to talk to Dr. Pevnick first. You knew that…"

"Yes, but the media already knows something. They're not buying the methane story anymore."

"They were last night. What happened? Who leaked the truth?"

Proger hesitated, then, "I don't know, sir. But it's out there. I think we need to talk about evacuation as well, sir."

"Absolutely not, Stan. Not until I talk with Dr. Pevnick. We already know that will cause widespread panic, food and fuel hoarding, armed robbery, looting, assaults. Total mayhem. That will be a last option for us, and I won't initiate evacuation until we have some armed forces in place to assist. Besides, I'm still hoping we will be able to do something with that fault line." He paused, rubbing his face. "Damn. I thought we could pull this off, at least until we had a better plan."

"Yes, sir."

Cooper stood up and hurriedly began to get dressed. He looked in the mirror. He needed a shave and to wash up. His face was swollen from sporadic sleep; he looked like he'd been up all night partying like a frat boy.

"Stan, I need you to do the press conference."

"Uh, of course, sir. What should I tell them?"

"Just stall. Tell them I had to rush to Camp David to meet with some people on this crisis. Tell them I will conduct a full press conference tomorrow morning at eight. Maybe I can find a positive spin to put on it by then."

"Okay, sir. I'll handle it." Proger heard the President hang up the phone. He smiled, looking down at his own phone and the recording device that was hooked up to it. "Gotcha," he said.

Cooper leaned back, wondering why Proger had called a press conference without conferring with him first. He felt uneasy. He'd been having a dream just before the phone had woke him up.

In the dream, he was standing on the Truman balcony of the White House, looking out toward the Washington monument. Below, he could see his daughter playing on the lawn. He looked back up to see a wall of water rushing into the city. It toppled the monolithic monument and came forth like a biblical curse. He felt a pang in the pit of his stomach as the lives, the lessons, the experiences, the archives of the great city, the home of the nation's history, all was wiped away. He felt a gripping fear when he looked back to his daughter and began to shout, "Run, run, run!" But she could not hear him, and the water swelled, rose up, and consumed her, like a giant shark.

***

At the Beehive, a ray of light fell across James's face and woke him. He pushed himself up off the table, one side of his face completely numb. He rubbed it briskly, trying to wake himself. He looked around, saw Etta and he smiled. Reaching over, he stroked her hair, softly, not wanting to wake her. The flickering of the computer screen caught his attention. There was an emergency webcast about to begin.

James watched the screen as Vice President Proger walked out to a stand of microphones. He looked authoritatively at the group of gathered reporters that hummed like bees. James turned the volume up on the computer and leaned forward, entranced.

"Thank you all for coming," said Proger. "What I'm about to say is going to be upsetting, understandably. Please listen to me, then I'll try to answer questions as best as I can." He paused and glanced solemnly at the faces of the reporters, then continued, "As you are all aware, approximately four days ago there was an explosion off the coast of the southeastern United States. Initially, it was thought best by *some* members of this administration to cover up the truth and report that the explosion was the result of a field of frozen methane that erupted."

The reporters murmuring grew louder, and Proger waited until it subsided. "As your Vice President, I can no longer stand by this falsehood and the indecisive planning that has become commonplace for this administration, leaving our country vulnerable to this type of attack. And so, I've decided to be open and honest with the American people. The facts are these: the explosion was a nuclear device and was the result of a terrorist act. Worse, the explosion was located at an unstable geographic site that is now quickly deteriorating and will soon cause an earthquake and resultant tidal wave that will endanger most of the eastern coast."

An audible gasp came from the phalanx of reporters that trickled off to silence again.

Proger continued, "In spite of my pleadings to establish an immediate emergency plan that would include mass evacuations of all coastal residents at least fifty to one hundred miles inland, as well as completely vacate the state of Florida, nothing has been done…until now. To allow you, the American people, to decide how we are going to survive this crisis, I offer my suggested plan:

"One: begin the evacuation of the eastern coastal states aided by our military, which in its depleted condition due to foreign commitments, will be supplemented by the able-bodied state militias that, historically, have been in existence since our forefathers wrote the Constitution of these great United States. Two: in order to maintain government order and leadership, I am asking all congressional members and the governors of each state to convene in St. Louis, because of its central and protected location, so that we can formulate a decisive and reasonable recovery plan for this, our country's greatest crisis ever. This planning session will include considering a complete overhaul of our nation's economy, so that we will not only survive this crisis, but we will recover our global economic standing. And, three: I am calling for an immediate investigation as to why the President has failed to take any steps toward mitigating this national disaster, and demand this investigation begin with the immediate impeachment of the President for negligence of his sworn duties. Now, please listen to this."

Proger stepped back and nodded to an aid on the side. There was a crackle across the public address system, then a recorded conversation:

"Stan, I need you to do the press conference." It was the President's voice.

"Of course, sir. What should I tell them?" Proger's response.

"Just stall. Tell them I had to go to Camp David."

"I think we need to talk about evacuation as well, sir."

"That will be a last option. Just stall. We…could pull this off…"

Proger returned to the bank of microphones. "I regret that I have had to bring this news to the American public, but I feel it is my sworn duty as Vice President and steward of the public trust to assure our government is transparent, proactive rather than reactive, and prepared to face any challenge that comes our way. Now, that is all I can say at this time. Please stay tuned to your televisions, radios, and computers for additional information on the mitigation of this threat to our great country."

A barrage of questions came from the reporters, some of whom ran up to the podium as if they were going to attack the Vice President. He waved them away. Pandemonium ensued, and several Secret Service agents rushed to keep the crowd back. Network cameras scanned the room. Most of the reporters, while normally quite cool, even in the blowing winds of a hurricane, had fear written on their faces, and the natural instinct for "flight or fight" was evident in all of them.

James stared at the screen in disbelief. He knew what this announcement would do to the psyche of all who saw it. He clenched his hands in prayer and closed his eyes. "God help us," he said out loud.

Within minutes of the announcement, cell towers were so jammed with calls that many people could not make connections at all. Television networks shut down all regular programming in order to pursue the story and sent armies of reporters into the field to investigate the disaster and to begin to cover the aftermath of the announcement. Stock markets fell. Riots and looting weren't far behind.

CHAPTER THIRTEEN

The sun glinted off the flawless black shine of the President's limousine as it tried to push through traffic. Even surrounded by the motorcade, their progress was stop-and-go through the D.C. gridlock.

Cooper wondered what the problem was as he used an electric shaver in the back seat. One of his closest advisors, Dr. Kevin Glass, a twenty-six-year-old Harvard graduate and already renowned economist, sat next to him. The young academic was tapping out numbers on his phone's calculator when it began vibrating.

"Good morning," said Glass inquisitively. He paused, his mouth falling open as he stared at the President. "What? I don't believe it. Are you sure?" His face was a mask of alarm.

Cooper raised his eyebrows in a silent question.

"It's the press secretary, sir," Glass explained, holding the phone momentarily away from his ear. "I'm afraid he has bad news. The Vice President just held a press conference and…"

"Yes," said Cooper. "I asked him to cover for me." The look on Glass's face suggested things had not gone according to plan. "What? What's happened?"

"I…well…uh…," said Glass, his face red as if it might explode.

Cooper grabbed the phone out of Glass's grasp. "This is the President," he growled. "What's going on? *What*? Why would he…? That fool! I just talked to him this morning. I thought he seemed… odd. What? He said 'impeach'? On what grounds?" There was a pause as he digested the message. "And what is Congress saying? Uh-huh. Okay. Stand by the phone. I'll be in touch."

Cooper leaned forward and turned on the television monitor in the back seat of the car. There were newscasts on every channel covering the Vice President's message and interviewing various congressmen. A reporter from NBC caught an elderly statesmen, Senator Martin from North Carolina. The reporter stuck a microphone in his face as the senator tried to dodge around him.

"Senator Martin, Senator Martin....would it be fair to say the government has been hiding this crisis from the American people?"

"Yes," the senator answered, visibly annoyed, "as well as from members of Congress. This morning was the first I've heard of a terrorist event. We should have begun evacuating three days ago."

"Obviously you have a lot of planning to do, as we all do, but can you comment on impeachment? Is that something Congress will consider for the President?"

"I'm not going to comment on that subject until I've met with my colleagues. As you know we are all on our way to an emergency Congressional meeting we were summoned to a few minutes ago. Our immediate priority is, of course, the safety and well-being of the citizens of this great country." Senator Martin considered his words carefully. "But," he continued, "if we need a change of leadership to deal with this crisis, then I, personally, would not rule out considering impeaching the President."

Cooper was outraged. "I knew that idiot didn't agree with me on how to handle this crisis but I never thought he'd go this far. "This is nothing less than a political coup, Kevin. And, under the circumstances, it might just work for him. I have to find out what he's up to. Can you get him on the phone for me?"

"I've been trying to, sir," said Glass. "He isn't answering."

"I see. Okay. I can't worry about Congress right now. Do me a favor, call any Congressman you're close to that you can trust. Tell them the truth about what we're trying to do. Find out where they stand. I'll have my secretary and her staff begin to do the same. Maybe we can get this turned around or, at least slow the fuse on the bomb, so to speak."

"Yes, sir," said Glass with enthusiasm.

"I've got to get in touch with Director Finney and make sure we have our emergency plan in place."

Glass nodded. "I'm sure you'll find you still have a lot of support, sir," he said, trying to put a positive spin on the dark moment.

Cooper glanced at him and shook his head. "Then you don't know politics yet, kid."

Glass began making phone calls, his fingers punching buttons like a machine.

Cooper leaned back, kneading his temples with his fingertips. His phone was in his lap—he knew he needed to start using it, and quick—but he was overwhelmed as he gazed out the window of the car and looked at the clouds in the sky. As he stared at one of them, he could swear it looked like a skull grinning at him.

CHAPTER FOURTEEN

Jeremy Clemens: Acquired Savant

Six years ago: Rouen, France

Jeremy squinted into the sunlight, waiting for the pitch. He enjoyed baseball, probably because his father liked it so much. If supporting the family as a mechanic hadn't been a priority, Jeremy knew his father would love to have been a professional baseball player. He used to tell the story that, if he had kept playing, he would have gone to the United States and joined the major leagues. That had been his dream.

Jeremy was fascinated with the engines and other things that his father repaired or rebuilt. He would watch him as he toiled over the engine compartment or under the car and hand him various tools. He wouldn't have minded being a mechanic like his father, but his father told him he would never allow that; Jeremy was going to go to school, then to college, and be the first one in his family to do so. There, he would study engineering or medicine or law, all highly respected professions that did not require one to constantly scrape the grease out from under one's fingernails with a pen knife, or smell like diesel fuel so strongly that not even two showers could erase the scent. Jeremy didn't mind the grease or the scent, and he enjoyed the sound of the engines when they ran smoothly, efficiently.

His mother worked cleaning houses. She didn't like her job either. She had always wanted to be an artist, but her family could not afford to send her to art school. So, she did what her mother did and her mother before that. Generations of cleaners.

"Strike One," yelled the umpire behind him. Though it was only minor league for twelve-year-olds, the man seemed to take his job seriously. Jeremy realized he'd been day dreaming. He shook himself out of it, twisted his torso back, lifting his shoulders slightly, and arched his left foot up, coiled and ready to nail the next one that came across the plate.

"Stay focused, Jeremy," hollered his father. He was behind the fence, near the dugout, within the corner of Jeremy's peripheral vision.

The pitcher began to wind up.

"Why don't you shut up and let the kid play," said another man, who stood up next to his father, sloshing beer from an open plastic cup. Jeremy tried not to look. But when he saw his father stand to argue with the man, he turned his head slightly to get a better look. The man pushed his father, and his father stumbled back. His mother put her hand over her mouth. That was the last thing Jeremy saw when he was "normal."

There was a nauseating crunch and a blinding flash of white light as the pitched ball hit him in the side of his head. Jeremy fell to the ground, his skull cracked. His eyes remained open, the pupil in one enlarging as the damage to his brain spread. Blood poured from his nose and ears. His eyes fixed on a giant clock that stood next to the scoreboard on the field. It read: 9:23am.

People ran to him: the coaches, his parents, other kids on his team. He could see them, but could not understand what they were saying...anymore. Then, the light went out, and he felt himself fall into a blackness in which he would remain for months.

At the hospital, Jeremy was assessed, and the prognosis was not good. His skull was shattered and blood was filling up inside, causing pressure on his brain. He would die soon, if the doctors did not remove a section of his skull. He might die, anyway. He had already stopped breathing, and was being kept alive on a ventilator. Jeremy's parents told the doctors to do what they could to save him. He was wheeled into an emergency room within forty minutes of the time he was standing at home plate waiting for that pitched ball.

The surgeons removed a circular section of his skull on the side where the baseball had struck him. The brain immediately swelled and pushed out of the hole the doctors had created, like dough rising quickly from a mixing bowl. They placed ice around his head and pushed pure oxygen into the tube inserted into his trachea. When the brain kept swelling, the surgeons removed part of it.

The piece of the skull they removed was kept in an isotonic solution, and when the surgeons were sure his brain had stopped swelling, the section was placed back onto Jeremy's head, like a missing puzzle piece. They sewed the skin back over it, leaving an oblong scar that looked like a halo tilted to one side.

The doctors told his parents they would have to wait and see. His chances were not good and, if he *did* survive, there would be severe damage. But, they could not say to what extent. He might not be able to walk, or even talk again. Time would tell.

When he awoke from a coma a few months later, Jeremy's body had shrunk from not moving his muscles, but he could move. Moreover, he could talk. His first words were: "Eet ees 9:23 am."

Those were the only words he could say for the first several weeks, as he embarked on an arduous regimen of physical therapy and struggled to learn to walk again. One day, when the nurses took him to the exercise room, they gave him a lump of clay to help him develop some hand-eye coordination. Jeremy stared at the clay, but did not see it as a lump; he saw it as an animal—a horse, in fact— though he had never actually seen a horse at that time.

The sound of the nurses' voices disappeared as he began to mold the clay. The only sounds he heard were from the machines surrounding him and the other patients. He could hear the cold air coming through the vents of the air conditioner, the belts inside of it that turned the fan, the chemicals that moved through its pipes. He could hear the pumping sounds of ventilators, like robotic breathing, and the whirr of bike sprockets and belts and beeps from the rehab machines.

When he could hear the nurses again, they were standing in front of him, gawking at the small but perfect horse that stood between his hands. "Did you make that, Jeremy?" one asked. "Have you done sculpture before?" He could understand them, but, when he tried to answer, all he could tell them was the time—the current time—three time zones away, over and over again.

Jeremy learned to talk over the next two years, though his speech pattern would forever be altered with repetitive phrases, interspersed with announcements of the exact time, usually several zones away. He joined a gym. There, he lifted incredible weights until he became a mass of muscles, which was a good thing; people did not make fun of him. He worked with his father in the mechanic shop. There was no mechanical problem that he could not fix, though he usually worked alone as his social skills did not develop beyond those of an adolescent. And he continued his sculptures, but they grew to a larger scale, and slowly, the organic subjects he used to sculpt became more and more mechanical. He began showing them in art galleries, when one well-known reviewer commented, "Clemens is an artist whose work is so original, it is uncompromisingly unique. His work blends an unusual combination of organic and mechanical forms that causes the viewer's mind to subtly twist. It is easy to imagine the sculptures are either a life form that is becoming a machine, or a machine that is starting to breathe. Thus, Clemens makes a discernible statement about what we are as a civilization and perhaps what we are becoming."

Jeremy had no idea what he was talking about.

CHAPTER FIFTEEN

In the piney woods of Pennsylvania, a horde of militia leaders gathered to meet with General Haufman and receive their orders. Behind them, scattered throughout the forest, were thousands of would-be soldiers. They came from all corners of the United States, deluded by a cause they felt was their right—their constitutional right—to not only question the government, but to change it, mold it into what they believed was right. They wore pseudo-military uniforms, mostly camouflage of varying types. Some wore the typical green, black, and brown swatched clothing. Some wore desert tan digitalized type, while others wore the forest pine type, popular with deer hunters. Still, many wore black SWAT type clothing. They all felt they were in proper military gear. The only common gear they wore was a grey corps ball cap, issued upon their arrival, that had a winged skull and the words "NEW U.S." embroidered across the crown. This distinction would be most important when they began occupying cities that, inevitably, would fall victim to chaos, looting, hoarding, and murder.

Haufman stood in front of them, standing in the bed of a military transport vehicle, a public address system in place. His own grey cap atop his head, uniquely adorned with four black stars across the brim. "Good morning, warriors!" he declared.

"Good morning, sir!" came back in a thunderous wave.

Haufman looked around, as if his gaze could meet the eyes of every man there.

"Men, the time has come for us to take back our country. The plans we have been laboring on for years will come to fruition within the next few days. We must be prepared. We will be facing a disaster, the likes of which this great nation has never seen, and for which few have prepared." He paused for effect, and to let the applause die down, then went on, "But, we *have* prepared. We have trained and waited for a time when we could offer our services and our devotion to this great country and its original Constitution. That time is now."

A cheer went out that echoed through the valleys. Farmers and residents in the area, believing a military training session was taking place, looked up but were not alarmed. There had been military exercises within the government-owned area previously. Locals believed they were safe and secure and even found comfort by the Army's presence. They could not have known this was not the Army or any other sanctioned group of Armed Forces.

Haufman continued, "Yes, there will be losses. But, we will not face them alone. Now, we have an ally, a leader who wants to see the changes we want to see. Vice President Proger will be our new President. He is with us, and he will be the strength we have wanted for our nation for years. Together, we will create a New Dawn for this country that our forefathers fought to hold free." Loud cheers and applause filled the air again.

"Our strategy will be this, gentlemen," the general went on. "We will align our forces along the outer perimeter of the hazard zone until flooding has subsided. While survivors and their weak leaders are scrambling around looking for help, we will move in and we *will* help them. While civil unrest continues, we will restore order by taking and holding local governments, until President Proger has realigned the nation's leadership. We are going to meet resistance from our brother soldiers, at least initially. Do what you have to do to hold our ground. We anticipate many of these soldiers will join us when they see the new leadership that President Proger offers. However, make no mistake: those who choose not to join us will be terminated with extreme prejudice. There will be no tolerance for traitors in our new nation."

Haufman gazed out across the sea of men, looking up as if talking to God. "Operation New Dawn begins now!"

A cheer went up that could actually be felt in the ground, like the first rumble of an earthquake.

"Before you gather your troops and move into place," Haufman said, once the crowd grew quiet, "I have something to show you." With no further explanation, Haufman leapt from the transport truck to the ground with surprising agility and strode toward the forest. "Follow me!" he commanded, motioning to his soldiers.

Slowly, the horde moved behind him as he led the way down a path behind his makeshift stage that widened into a clearing, then rose up a hill. Standing at the top, he waited until a majority of the men could align with him at the crest. Some of them saw what he wanted them to see into the valley below, and murmuring began, erupting in a buzz of conversation like bees forming a hive. Some of the men high-fived each other, while others pointed and shook their heads in disbelief. Their dreams were coming true.

Like a proud parent on Christmas morning, the general again addressed his troops. "I told you President Proger was with us. To show his encouragement and his good faith, he's given us a few presents!" Haufman waved his arm out, like Moses parting the Red Sea. The field below was filled with armament. Tanks, cannons, missiles, Hummers, personnel and weapons transports stretched out before them. "This," he announced, ending his speech with both fists raised in the air, "is the strength of our New Dawn!"

CHAPTER SIXTEEN

James entered the workshop that stood surrounded, almost hidden, by dense brush in the rear acreage of the Beehive facility. The scent of blueberries filled the early afternoon air. Inside the shop, however, it smelled of sawdust and machine oil and rodent musk. James's nose twitched as he let his eyes adjust to the dim light inside.

Jeremy was finishing mechanical adjustments on a small, unusual looking machine. It appeared to be a gun of sorts, like a small cannon. Made of a combination of shiny chrome and rusted parts, it culminated in a cylindrical barrel, with a gleaming gem attached at the tip. To James, it could've been a poorly made replica of a ray gun used in an old serial movie, like Flash Gordon or Buck Rogers. An array of wires ran away from it and attached to a small bank of solar panels.

Etta worked quietly in the corner of the shop, leaning over a large sketch pad on a table; a rusty, old coffee can filled with sharpened pencils sat nearby.

"Hello," said James in his thick English accent. "What have we here?"

Harvey abruptly barged in. "Etta asked me to look up su...su...some...*cuss, cuss*, eh, information about lasers. Uh, at least I think that's what she asked me."

James looked at Etta quizzically.

Etta smiled and nodded vigorously.

Harvey went on, "I found everything I could, literally everything there is available on the subject of lasers, and discovered that with the right power source, you can build your own homemade lasers. Just like in the James Bond movies. Even better, we already had most of the parts on our solar vehicle."

James saw what was left of the solar tractor they'd built the day before. It was reduced to a pile of spare parts and looked as if giant metal-eating rats had fed upon it. He turned to Etta and spoke in Japanese. "Why a laser?"

Etta shrugged and smiled demurely at him, but didn't answer.

James looked at the faces of the rest of the crew. "You know, I think Dr. Pevnick wanted those solar panels back."

Harvey shrugged, too, and scratched mindlessly at his groin.

Jeremy looked guilty and tried to turn away and busy himself with something else, but there was nothing else. He turned back to Etta, and said, "Eet ees as you designed, Etta." Then added, "Eet ees 2:39 in Sao Paulo."

Etta nodded and looked back to James, then tilted her chin toward the small machine.

"Okay," said James. "Let's see if it works, shall we?"

Etta went to one of the windows in the workshop and drew back a heavy curtain that shielded the milky glass. A wave of dust fell from the drapes and glowed in the shaft of sunlight coming through the window. Etta stood in the light and, for a breathtaking moment, it appeared as if she had a halo around her dark head of hair. She nodded to Jeremy, who flicked some switches and pushed some buttons on a small, handheld remote control.

An intense red light appeared at the tip of the miniature cannon, like a bright red lipstick emerging from its case. A reflection of the red light appeared on the wall.

"So, you've all been out here building a rather fancy pointer?" asked James, sardonically.

There was an old, cracked mirror lying on a workbench in the shop and Etta picked up a shard of it. She sidled over to the window where a weak ray of sunlight managed to push through the clouded glass. Angling the mirror in the light, she maneuvered its reflection onto the solar panel powering the small cannon. The crystal tip grew brighter and redder, and the machine began to make a humming noise.

James watched as the tiny red dot on the wall began to emit a small wisp of smoke, then more curled up as the light grew brighter. A bright white flame appeared, then grew as the wall opened, deteriorating under the intense heat of the beam. James could actually see beyond the shop wall as the beam made its way through and began to incinerate a bush outside. The laser cannon hummed loudly, shuttering under its own power. Then, it sputtered, made popping sounds, and its beam went dark. The crystal glowed for a moment before turning a deep, blood red.

"That was...*cuss, cuss*, awesome!" said Harvey.

"Yes, it was," admitted James. "What is that crystal at the tip of the laser?"

"What is zee crystal? What is zee crystal? Tip. Tip. Tip. Well, eet ees zee diamond. Oui?"

"And where did you get a diamond?" James inquired.

Jeremy looked at Harvey for an answer, grimacing, turning the corners of his mouth down. Harvey looked at Etta, who in turn, looked down and shrugged again. This promoted a round of laughter, until even James had to smile.

Jeremy was the first to stop laughing as he looked out the window and saw something. The others ran to the window to see the President's motorcade pull into the facility grounds again, dust billowing from the tires crunching over the gravel entry.

"Ah," said Harvey. "The king is back."

CHAPTER SEVENTEEN

Dr. Pevnick stepped out of the shower and wrapped himself in a familiar and comfortable terry cloth robe. There were days when he thought he could still smell his wife's scent on it. This was one of those days. He was shaving, remembering how she used to teasingly mock the faces he made in the mirror as he slid the blade down his cheek, when he heard the knock on his bedroom door. Dropping his razor and reaching for a towel to wipe his hands, he stepped through the room and opened the door to the hall to find Mrs. Brown standing there. She was dressed nice, rather than her usual business-like attire, as if she were going out to a formal, late lunch. From her ears dangled exquisite earrings, though Pevnick noticed one of them was missing a diamond.

"Did you get some rest, professor?" she asked.

"A little," he said, a drop of water leaking from his curled locks and trailing through the shaving cream on his face.

"I hope it was enough," she said, tacitly. "The President is here."

"Already?"

"He's in your office. I made him tea."

"Thank you. I'll be right there." He turned to finish shaving, then turned back. "Oh, eh, by the way…you're missing a diamond from your earring," he said, his eyes focusing on the left one.

Mrs. Brown jerked her hand up to her ear, surprised. "Oh, dear. So I am."

Pevnick finished up in the bathroom and hurried to his office, grabbing some papers along the way. President Cooper stood as he entered the room, and Pevnick handed him his completed report.

"Thank you, Stephen," said Cooper. "I'm sure you've done an excellent job, in spite of the lack of time. Now, let's have a seat. Mrs. Brown has been kind enough to set up a conference call for me with some of my advisors in Washington, and I've asked Mr. Tramwell to join us."

Pevnick thought he'd heard wrong. "James?" he asked.

"Yes," the President answered. "He said something yesterday that got me thinking. I ran it by several of the scientists who are in my confidence, and they agreed with what he was saying."

"About making the mass smaller, thereby decreasing the force?" James asked, as he boldly entered the room.

"Why, yes," answered Cooper. "Hello, James. Please join us."

"Thank you, Mr. President." James took a seat and opened a laptop he brought with him. A voice came over the speaker, indicating the conference call was starting.

"Hello, Dr. Hisamoto here…"

"…and Dr. Heimel here…"

"Welcome gentlemen, and thank you," said Cooper. "I'm here with Dr. Stephen Pevnick at his research center. I know you are aware of his reputation in behavioral sciences. Also joining us is Mr. James Tramwell. He is a renowned mathematician."

"I've read some of your research, Mr. Tramwell. Really amazing material."

"Thank you, Dr. Hisamoto," said James, beaming. "I've read your work, too."

James glanced at Pevnick, who smiled back at him and gave him a 'thumbs up.'

"Well, then," said Cooper, "let's get to it. I've asked you gentlemen here to discuss our situation. We've all agreed that if we can remove some of the shelf along the fault line, we could possibly reduce its force when it fails."

"Agreed," said Heimel.

"Yes," said Hisamoto.

"Okay," said Cooper, "I've moved the Navy into position along the fault and they're preparing to do whatever is necessary when we give them the order. Now, I've got some ideas from Doctors

Hisamoto and Heimel, but I wanted everyone to hear Mr. Tramwell's thoughts. James?"

"Right, then," James began, taking a deep breath. "I've anticipated this discussion, Mr. President, and I've drawn up some figures and graphs I'll forward on to your team. I've also put together an animation sequence of what I'm going to suggest, so we can all follow along easily." He fidgeted with his laptop and shuffled some papers before stacking them neatly next to him. He took a deep breath, then began, "Basically, my suggestion is for your submarines to fire low-impact torpedoes into the fault shelf. The torpedoes can be modified per some suggestions that my team—Etta, Harvey, and Jeremy—have designed, basically using your Mark 54 Lightweight Hybrid model, but reducing the explosive to approximately one-quarter of what it normally is. Or, we could replace the warhead, altogether, with highly compressed air; an idea untried, yes, but one I like better. We need to crumble the wall, not blow it to kingdom come and possibly exacerbate the problem.

Hisamoto pursed his mouth and nodded, then took out a mechanical pencil and began to scribble some figures on a pad.

Heimel frowned and blinked his eyes repeatedly as if trying to make some calculations in his head, before he withdrew a calculator from an inside pocket of his coat and began punching at the keys.

James looked at Pevnick for reassurance and the professor gave him a slight nod to continue.

"The Australians utilize the Mark 54, as well as the U.S. Navy, in case we need more of them. We don't have time for manufacturing, so these torpedoes could do the job for us with little modification as early as tomorrow."

"I see," said Cooper. "Is that what you were thinking, Dr. Hisamoto?"

"Uh, yes, sir," Hisamoto replied, looking back and forth between his own scribbled figures and James's data. "More or less."

"Dr. Heimel?" said Cooper.

"Yes, sir. Dr. Hisamoto and I have been over this scenario numerous times since we met last night. We put it before a group of scientists we believe to be the best in the world as a hypothetical problem and, given the circumstances, we feel it is the best alternative. But, we...don't all agree where the detonations should take place. Primarily, our lack of agreement comes from not knowing where the weakest areas of the fault line are; that is, the areas most likely to trigger an instant failure."

"I understand," said James. "I've consulted with my colleague, Etta Kim, on this subject. If you don't know her, she is a genius in ocean engineering, I can assure you. She, *we*, feel that the weakest sections are the areas where the fault line is most vertical. However, we both feel these are the areas in which we need to concentrate the detonations."

There was silence for a moment before Dr. Heimel began to speak again, "I see," he said. "But, in doing that, won't we risk upsetting the apple cart, so to speak?"

"Of course," James answered, opening his presentation and turning his laptop so the President could see. "But we don't see much of a choice." On the screen, animated graphics showed a line of submarines spread along the fault line at regular intervals. Each fired a torpedo, succeeded by a second torpedo. The fault line shelf crumbled from one end to the other in a seemingly orderly fashion.

"The fault could fail at any moment," James continued. "If we go with the alternative and detonate an area we believe to be the least likely to fail, what good are we doing? A blast in what we might even consider to be a safe area could cause a failure, and what would we have accomplished? We believe our best option is to chip away at the most vertical areas of the shelf. If it fails, we might accelerate the progress of the event. But, if it holds—even for a day or two, allowing removal of even a fraction of its mass—then we will have succeeded in reducing the mass, which will reduce the force. At least partially."

"Hmm," Dr. Hisamoto contemplated. "I see what you're saying. But, I think I'd like to hear Ms. Kim's thoughts as well. I've read her articles on ocean tectonics, and I would like to hear if she has considered alternatives."

James looked at Dr. Pevnick and shook his head.

Pevnick had to agree. "I don't think that will be possible," he said. "If you've read her work, you might be familiar with her, eh, *affliction*, which prevents her from communicating in a group forum."

There was silence in the room. It seemed everyone was

uncomfortable with the choice of Pevnick's word, *affliction*, particularly James.

"I...see," said Hisamoto. "So, what's our next step? Are we to make our decision based on the theory of one, er, uh...?"

"Savant?" James quipped.

"Well..." said Hisamoto, at a loss for words.

"Excuse me, gentlemen," said Cooper. "But, the final decision rests on me. I've heard enough to convince me we have to do something, and there are risks no matter which way we choose to proceed; nature does not lend any guarantees. A few days ago, I asked for solutions, and none were forthcoming. With almost every theory in science, there is another that opposes it. I've seen as much wrong born of indecision as I have from making the wrong decision. I listened to this young man's proposal, watched him present it to the scientific community, and only then did I hear we *might* be able to do something." He paused, waiting for a response—any response. None came.

"We all agree we have to do *something*," the President went on. "If we learned just one thing from Katrina, it *is* that. Dr. Hisamoto and Dr. Heimel, I am going to ask you to stay in touch with Mr. Trammel. Work together, but keep this in mind: Mr. Trammel will be the lead on this team whose focus will be the science part of the project. You will all work with the Directors of Homeland Security and the Defense Department. Am I clear on this?"

"Yes, sir," said Hisamoto.

"Of course," said Heimel.

"Now," Cooper stood and finished his delivering his orders, "I am going to keep this line open for you and James to continue this discussion. I'll contact my Department Directors, and ask them to join in on the call. You gentlemen will be directing the Navy through them and our land-based Ops center. I'll repeat," he said, his eyes sweeping the room, "this is a team effort. Dr. Pevnick and I are going to discuss evacuation strategies. Then, I'm going to hold a press conference and tell the nation we have a plan before my detractors can cause any more widespread panic. I'll ask all of you to keep our discussions confidential until I say it's safe to do otherwise. Everyone understand?"

A general rumbling of affirmative responses concluded the

conversation. The President signaled for Pevnick to follow him out of the room. They made their way toward the kitchen for coffee. Mrs. Brown had a small television set on and was watching the news with obvious concern on her face, her hands clasped below her chin as if in prayer.

The news showed a park ranger being interviewed. He reported that he'd noticed animals leaving their dens and headed for the mountains, and added, "They head for the high ground when they sense danger." Another report showed clips of whales washing up on the beaches in staggering amounts. Each following report only added to the dread they were all feeling.

Pevnick turned off the set before pouring coffee for himself and Cooper. He reached over and took Mrs. Brown's hands and rubbed the back of them with his fingers while he looked into her face. "Try not to worry about things we have no control over, okay?"

Mrs. Brown nodded, and her eyes became wet. "Please let me get that for you, gentlemen," she said, rising to her feet. "Wasn't it cream and sugar, Mr. President?"

CHAPTER EIGHTEEN

From the air, the hidden bunker looked like a small rise in the ground; a hill surrounded by lush forest growth. Nothing to draw suspicion. Inside, the newest technology in communications lined the curved walls that ran the length of a football field and equaled anything that the Pentagon was using, primarily because most of the design of the bunker had come from the Pentagon, stolen by trusted members of the government.

General Haufman sat with almost one hundred of his closest "Generals," most of whom were not real generals, at all, merely heads of various statewide militias and delegates from each of the state's extreme political factions. They were listening to President Cooper's discussion with several world-renowned scientists. It was supposed to be a confidential conversation. Haufman could barely disguise his enthusiasm as he made a call.

"Sir," he said into the phone, "the bug our man planted is working well. We just listened to Cooper's meeting with the scientists and that group at the nuthouse research facility. They have a plan that the President is going to present at a press conference as soon as they have their evacuation strategy finalized."

On the other end of the line, Vice President Proger responded, "We anticipated this," he said. "But right now he's having a credibility problem. People are panicking already. Gas and water hoarding has begun. The interstates and turnpikes are filling with cars headed west. Grocery and hardware stores are quickly running out of supplies, and the police can't keep up with the looting. No one is going to stop self-evacuating to listen to a president they believe misled them and imperiled their lives. Let's proceed as planned. Begin placing the militias where we need them."

Haufman nodded to his collected staff, silently clenching his fist and holding it up to them in a gesture of strength. They looked pleased and began to shake hands with each other.

"I've been talking with the Department of Defense staff," Proger continued. "Other than the director, I think I have them listening to me and they're convinced the President is frozen with indecision and gone into hiding. His silence right now is only confirming that. Even his allies are abandoning him. The generals tell me there is no way they'll be able to get a sufficient number of troops back on U.S. soil in time to sustain a force and control a mass exodus of people fleeing the coastal regions.

"But," he continued, "be advised they are mobilizing the National Guard and all stateside forces. And, we still have the Air Force to contend with, but I'm working on that."

"Understand, sir, and I agree. There's no way they can pull together an opposing force fast enough to be any threat to us.

"Then, as of now," said Proger, "Operation New Dawn is under way, General."

Haufman hung up the phone and gave one command: "Mobilize."

***

Etta walked along the rim of a cliff overlooking the ocean. She had been so nervous, she'd begun stimming again, almost uncontrollably. Now, with the sea breeze pushing salt-scented, fresh air into her nostrils, she calmed down. She breathed deeply, feeling the air's healing abilities and the tranquil peace it lent her.

Harvey and Jeremy bumped along the path behind her, trying to give her the time she needed to regain her calm. They glanced repeatedly back over their shoulders, up toward the house, where the President and his motorcade of Secret Service vehicles spread across the lawn like a flock of crows come to ground. Harvey noticed glints of sunlight beaming off several sets of binoculars trained on them as they took their walk.

"Son's of…," Harvey began.

"Eh, eh," said Jeremy, surprisingly diplomatic. "Zee cussing, Harvey. By the way, it ees 7:15pm in Geneva."

Harvey turned red with displaced anger. "Who gives a flying fu…fu…*frog* what time it is in France?" he blurted. "Buncha cheese-loving wino snobs." Then, remembering Jeremy was from France, he cooled and added, "I was just going to say sons of beaches, anyway."

Jeremy shrugged as they continued their stroll and caught up to Etta.

"Are you well, Mademoiselle? Well, Mademoiselle?" asked Jeremy, falling back into his pattern of repeating phrases. They were all stressed out, worrying about the plan they had offered, and like everyone else on the east coast, what might happen to them in the next few days.

Etta shook her head. In her tiny voice, she said, "It is all so big. We…don't know if it will work."

"Yes," said Harvey, trying to put a positive spin on the conversation, "but we know what will happen if we don't try something, right?" He moved up beside her and, for one of the few times in his life, felt the need to give another comfort and placed his arm over her shoulders.

Jeremy, watching the gesture, moved to her other side and did the same; his huge, muscled arm overlapping Harvey's. Between the two of them, they were almost crushing her, but she stood erect and took their added weight. She closed her eyes and felt the sun on her face.

"Thank you for being my friends," she said.

"It is our pleasure," said Harvey.

"*Oui, oui, oui,*" said Jeremy.

Then Harvey burst out laughing so hard he had to bend over and place his hands on his knees, audibly wheezing. Pointing at Jeremy, he said, "That…ha, ha…sounded like a pig! You know, like the little pig who ran all the way home, saying *oui, oui, oui…*"

Etta looked at Jeremy and frowned.

Jeremy let out a booming laugh of his own. Then, Etta began to laugh; her voice sounding brittle and delicate, like miniature bells.

"It's good to hear you laugh," said James. He had come up from the other side of the trail, surprising them all. He was wearing dark sunglasses with leather blinders along the sides of them, like polar explorers wear. They helped keep him from getting distracted. He was freshly bathed and wearing cologne he'd borrowed from Dr. Pevnick, something he'd never done before.

Etta turned and smiled at him, her cheeks flushing.

"I just remembered I have to finish reading a book on the aftermath of Mount Vesuvius," said Harvey. "Shouldn't take more than a few minutes, but it's a very well researched tome." He looked at Jeremy and moved his eyebrows around, twitching his head not so discreetly to one side in an effort to urge Jeremy to follow.

Instead, Jeremy smiled at him in wonder.

"Ahem," said Harvey, attempting a Plan B. "Didn't you say you could fix my cell phone for me, Jeremy? The alarm function doesn't seem to be working."

"Oh…oui," said Jeremy, finally getting it. "Of course, let us go feex your phone."

James nodded to them, and idled up to Etta. "Hi."

"Hello, James. You look…nice. And you *smell* nice, too."

James gave a crooked smile. "You look lovely today, too, Etta." He reached out his hand and took hers. She didn't resist.

"Wanna walk some more?" James asked.

Etta nodded, looking up into his face. "It is a nice day for it."

They walked quietly for a while, holding hands like an old couple who had been doing it for years. The path followed downhill and came to the edge of thick woods, filled with long since abandoned maples and wild blueberries and apple trees, survivors from a time when the land was used for farming. Their fresh, sweet scent was intoxicating and magical to two people whose senses were so enhanced.

Once under the canopy of the forest, James stopped and gently turned Etta toward him.

She looked up into his face, the shadows of the leaves were like silk-screened images on her skin, and he could not believe how incredibly beautiful she was…so exotically perfect. Her raven hair glinted in the sunlight, framing her face, her incredibly huge eyes drawing him in. The perfect symmetry of her face was particularly alluring to him, everything in exact mathematical proportion:

small ears to small nose to small mouth, with full, impossibly pink lips that withdrew into her mouth and came back out shining wet. All exactly matched, except for those eyes, which were almost extraterrestrial in their enormous size. In the chocolate brown of the irises, James noted shards of amber bursting out from the pupils. He tried not to count them. Even her eyelashes were precisely balanced—and these he *did* count, he couldn't help himself—and they were symmetrically balanced, with one hundred and two lashes on the upper lids, and forty-eight lashes on the bottom, on both sides. He'd never felt this way about another person before, and he felt a flutter in his stomach.

Detecting butterflies of her own, Etta was both nervous and near breathless with an excitement she had never experienced. At another time, she might have started the aggravating stimming that embarrassed her so. But, as James held her gaze, looking into her face, she could see the ocean in her peripheral vision. She could hear it, too, and—more importantly—she could *feel* the giant force of nature that tied into her body like plasma. Its presence soothed her as they drew in closer to each other.

"Etta," James almost whispered, "have you ever kissed…"

Etta cut him off as she leaned up on her tip-toes, placed her small, delicate hands around the back of his neck, and, using her arms like a soft scarf to pull his lips to hers, gently kissed him.

James kissed her back, more urgently, and pulled her into his arms. Her touch felt electric and, for the first time in both their lives, they felt an emotion both believed would forever be foreign to them: Love.

As they kissed, visions filled their minds. Etta thought of the ocean with warm waves washing over her, enveloping her, lending her the comfort that a fetus must feel in its mother's womb. James thought of patterns and mathematical designs and formations, like a flock of birds flying in an almost perfect isosceles triangle. While those figures gave him comfort, too, something emerged, or tried to emerge. And it was urgent. He struggled to put his finger on it, even as he enjoyed the first kiss of his life—*perhaps it was the perfect geometry found in nature*? But with the physicality of the embrace, the scent of the sun's warmth on Etta's hair and skin, the passion of the kiss…it was all too distracting for him to put together the arc of what the image was trying to tell him.

CHAPTER NINETEEN

President Cooper and Dr. Pevnick wrapped up their business and phone calls—as much as a President can to allow himself a few minutes of solace—and took a walk outside at Pevnick's suggestion. They noticed Etta and James walking back along a trail that overlooked the sea. They were holding hands.

"They're good kids," Cooper said. Then, contemplating his own words, changed that. "Good *people*, I guess I should say. Probably wouldn't be in our best interests if I told the American people that I was relying on the advice of individuals just out of their teens to save them all."

Pevnick nodded, but didn't say anything. He was wise enough to know when people simply needed to hear themselves talk. But, he made a mental note: *were James and Etta learning something else besides solar powered cars and trying to save the world? Could they be developing feelings for each other?* It was something he hadn't even considered when he'd made the decision to bring them together for a project.

"It's beautiful here," said Cooper, looking out over the ocean.

"Yes, sir, it is," said Pevnick.

"It's begun. The submarines are moving into place along the fault line. God help us."

Pevnick did not respond; he had nothing to add to that statement.

"Stephen, I've never been so...I've never had..."

"It's understandable, Jack," Pevnick awkwardly interrupted, still uneasy using the President's first name. "We're all pretty nervous right now. You have a lot on your shoulders. But, I think you're making the best decisions based on the circumstances."

"Time will tell."

"Are you still planning on the press conference today?"

Cooper stopped walking, turned and looked into Pevnick's face. "I've decided to wait until tomorrow. I want our mitigation efforts to be fully mobilized before I tell the world."

"Understood," said Pevnick, his face showing doubt.

"You think I should do it sooner, don't you?"

Pevnick shrugged. "I can't advise you on that. I just know that fear and the unknown breeds more fear and anxiety. People are already in a panic after the Vice President's announcement. By tomorrow, there is no telling what may happen."

Cooper nodded. "We might not even have a tomorrow, Stephen." He paused. "I think the American people are stronger, braver than we sometimes give them credit for. I'm going to wait until I have something more positive to tell them."

They walked toward the back of the property allowing James and Etta their privacy. The yard opened into an expansive field filled with tall, wheat-like grass. Groups of birds flew overhead.

Cooper looked up at them, and said, "Lately, it seems I've been seeing the beauty of nature more than usual. I don't remember ever seeing so many birds this time of year."

The two of them stopped their stroll again and watched as the birds landed on the branches of a nearby tree, filling it with color and commotion. Several deer appeared on top of a hill in the distance, and the two groups—man and animal—stood stock still, gazing at each other. The wind blew and patterns formed in the long grass like waves moving across the field. Clouds of all shapes and sizes filled the skies.

"Huh," said Cooper. "Does that cloud look like a question mark to you?"

"Yes," said Pevnick. "I suppose it does."

The two men stood there for an elongated silence.

"I'd like to ask a favor," said Cooper, turning to Pevnick. "Washington is too hot at the moment. I'd like to stay here this evening, if it wouldn't be too much of an imposition. I feel… closer to the problem here. Can you put me up?"

"Of course," said Pevnick, smiling. "I think we can find an extra sleeping bag around here for you."

Cooper laughed. "A few of my security people will stay here, too. I'll send the rest to hotels in town."

"As you wish, sir. We have plenty of room for your needs. C'mon. I'll go tell Mrs. Brown, and she can make arrangements."

***

On the bottom of the ocean, off the coast of North Carolina, the fault line suddenly opened and a mountain-sized chunk of its vulnerable lip crumbled, sending shock waves through the sea.

The S.S. Virginia, a State Class submarine, picked up the disturbance on their sonar only moments before the wave hit. They barely had time to brace themselves as the sea jolted them around like a carnival ride.

The captain of the sub, an experienced seaman of some thirty years, said, "Damn, we're still two miles away from ground zero, and we're getting that much turbulence. Hold steady men. Like Miss Bette Davis used to say, "'It's going to be a bumpy night.'"

A wide-eyed ensign, sweat dripping down the sides of his face, approached the commander once he was able to get his feet back under him. "Sir, do you think we are going to survive this operation?"

"You want me to be honest, son?"

"Yes, sir,"

"Hell, yes!" said the captain boldly. But, after the ensign had turned away, the captain's brave smile faded. His lieutenant commander approached and cleared his throat.

"You really believe that, sir?"

The captain contemplated before answering, then said, "No, sir. We don't have a chance in hell. But, we'll go down knowing we tried to save our country. Isn't that what we're here for? Now, make sure those torpedoes are scaled down to the specifications so we don't blow that fault wider than a politician's mouth."

The petty officer forced a smile and saluted his Captain. "Yes, sir!"

The captain watched the petty officer rush to fulfill his directive. His command had sounded strong—it had to be—as with any he issued, in order to get scores of men jacked up enough to be willing to sacrifice themselves. He was proud to be commanding these brave young men, but as the angry ocean begin to push against the ship, he felt a pang of sorrow that he was, in all likelihood, leading these men to their deaths.

CHAPTER TWENTY

In his dimly lit, aseptic room, Douglas Pevnick was filling the writing tablet with symbol after symbol, each flowing from one to the other, his hand feverishly moving over the surface of the pages with the pen he gripped in his clumsy, twisted fingers. He was sitting in front of the window, trying to keep his head and hands steady, slow their jerky motions, and record what he was *seeing* before the sun went down. Flocks of birds were filling the skies and trees, flying wildly, chaotically.

Suddenly, Douglas's eyelids began to flutter as his limbs became racked with the grip of a seizure. His neck arched back impossibly, as his jaws clinched and tremors took over his body, throwing him out of the wheelchair.

Squawking birds began propelling themselves against the window as Magritte, the nurse, came back into the room. "Oh, my," she said, alarmed. She knelt down next to Douglas, trying to calm him, initially, but she quickly identified the persistent seizures as status epilepticus and knew she would need medication to control them. She moved furnishings away from Douglas's writhing form so he would not hurt himself, and ran to the intercom on the wall. "Help!" she pleaded. "Mrs. Brown, someone! I need help in Douglas's room." Then she raced to the drawer and removed some medication and IV supplies.

James was bouncing through the house on his way back to his

room. He never felt more alive than at that very moment. He tried to concentrate on the figures he needed to complete his calculations, but the image of Etta, and the memory of her touch, her taste, distracted him. He didn't mind. She'd said she had work to do, too, but as they parted for their separate rooms, he sensed the shared knowledge they had discovered: they weren't alone, anymore; they had each other.

His cheeks were red, warmed by the sun and tinted with the blush of young love. His thoughts swirled around something he'd never felt before. It was another one of those things that could not be explained on paper with calculations. Another one of those things, you simply had to believe in.

His phone vibrated again. It was a group text from Dr. Hisamoto that included his name along with Heimel, several department directors, and *the President of the United States*! Energized with newfound confidence, James steered his mental focus to the calculations he needed to answer the persistent questions from the scientists who had now taken to calling or texting him, just like he was…what…*normal*? He pondered the implications of that thought and had just placed his hand on the door knob to his room when he heard the nurse's plea for help. He stopped, listening, trying to comprehend the meaning of the plea as Mrs. Brown pushed by, almost knocking him down in her rush.

"Excuse me, James," she called back, breathlessly.

James watched her speed down the hall. He frowned, wondering what the commotion was, then decided there was only one way to find out. He followed Mrs. Brown. Quickening his pace to catch up, he watched her dart into a room. Before the door shut behind her, he caught it, and eased into the doorway.

Across what could only be described as a bedroom turned into a makeshift hospital room, Mrs. Brown and Magritte crouched over a young man dressed in a patient's gown, trying to restrain him. He watched as the nurse fastened a tourniquet around the teenager's arm and struggled to start an IV as he tossed about. Mrs. Brown helped steady the arm as the catheter needle found its way into a bulging blue-green vein in the patient's pale skin.

James watched, fascinated—though he had experienced seizures for years, he'd never seen someone having one. He was about to say something when he noticed some notebook pages scattered about the room. Leaving the door ajar, he stepped toward the far window, bent over, and picked up one of the pages. Behind him, Dr. Pevnick threw open the door and burst into the room.

"James, please go away," he said, urgently.

James ignored him; instead, he watched as Pevnick knelt at the young man's side. He wondered who the young man was. Why hadn't Pevnick told them about him? He was obviously a patient; were there more? Looking around, James noticed several dead birds on the outside windowsill as he gathered more of the fallen pages. He was startled by what he found. Though the pages were filled with scribbles that no one else could possibly read, he *could*. They were messages—suggestions, calculations, and bold hypotheses—and they were addressed to *him*. James felt his heart beat faster as the enormity of what he was reading dawned on him.

"I'm sorry," said Magritte, "I just stepped out of the room for a moment. When I came back, he was like this."

"Did you take him outside?" Pevnick asked. "I advised you not to..." He stopped when he noted Mrs. Brown giving him a wordless, but scolding frown.

Magritte pushed Valium into the IV, and the seizures quickly began to subside. The young man's skin was soaked with sweat from the exertions.

Perspiring, too, Magritte finally looked up at Dr. Pevnick, her face stony. "No, sir," she said. "I did not take your son outside. He has been staring out this window since you left this morning. I've never seen him like this. He just keeps scribbling in that writing pad you put here."

"What pad?" asked Pevnick.

"This one," said James, holding it up, along with the loose pages, for him to see.

Pevnick rose to his feet and pushed back his hair, catching his breath. "It's...just doodles. He's having some unusual neurological activity today. That's all. He doesn't know what he's doing...but please, James. Please, go away. This...doesn't concern you."

James tilted his head quizzically. "Hmmm. I'm afraid it does. Did you tell your, uh...*son* that I was here?"

Pevnick frowned, wondering what he was getting at. "No, of

course not. He doesn't know who you are."

"Oh, but he does. You see, Dr. Pevnick, these scribbles, as you call them, are written in my own universal language, the *Manti* we discussed previously."

Pevnick's face twisted, incredulous. "What? No. You're mistaken..."

"Hardly, professor. This one in particular is addressed to me." James held up one of the pages as if he were an attorney in court, revealing crucial evidence. Then, edgy, he said, "We need to talk, sir."

Pevnick helped Mrs. Brown and Magritte lift Douglas and put him back into bed. He was exhausted, and his eyelids fluttered shut; his breathing slowed, his body loosened.

"You're right," said Pevnick, wiping a sheen of perspiration from his face with the sleeve of his jacket. "Yes, James. You're right. We need to talk."

CHAPTER TWENTY-ONE

An hour later, James was seated at a table in the study, piles of papers in front of him, along with several open books. A laptop flickered images of swirling patterns of dots, like Twentieth Century Op Art come to life.

Dr. Pevnick entered the room refreshed, but with a stern look on his face. "This will have to be quick, James. The President is going to do a live telecast from here in the morning. He's asked me to be there with him and to help prepare some notes tonight."

"Of course," said James, dryly. An awkward silence followed in which James continued scribbling on a notepad, looking through the pile of books, and watching his computer screen—immersed, as if Dr. Pevnick was not there.

Pevnick shuffled his feet, then mulled about the room as though seeing it for the first time. "I'm sorry you had to find out about Douglas like that," the doctor offered.

James looked up and stopped his research. "Me, too. It makes me...question your integrity."

Pevnick's face darkened. "I had my reasons for the deception... allowing people to believe he was dead."

"Yes, indeed," said James, standing. "Were you embarrassed you had a son—a *behavioral problem*—you couldn't fix?"

"That's not fair."

"Is he the reason you brought us here? Were you hoping to find a key, to see how we *defects*, or—what was your word—those with *afflictions* function?"

"No," Pevnick said, raising his voice, "I was trying to protect him. The reasons I brought you here had nothing to do with him."

James continued his work for a moment, dropping the conversation.

"I have to go," said Pevnick.

"Wait," said James, putting down his pad. "There's something you should know. The President will want to know this, too."

"Quickly," said Pevnick, impatient.

"Based on your son's writings…"

"His *what*?"

"Yes, doctor. His *writings*. He clearly knows the language that I believed *I* had made up. Evidently, I was not the original author of this language."

"Who was, or is, then?"

"This will be hard for you to follow, but I am going to ask you to bear with me, to take a leap of faith, if you will."

"Are you going to tell me Douglas made up this language?" he said, irritated. "That's impossible. The accident that killed my wife and left him…well, it left him with only part of his brain. The cognitive part doesn't exist anymore."

"Not unlike, let's say, a savant?" James asked. "Even with your perfunctory review of savants, you should know some of us operate, perhaps even excel, using only part of our brain."

Pevnick walked to the window of the study, peering out as if looking for an answer. Quietly, almost imperceptibly, he replied, "Yes. Yes. Of course. You're right. I did want to learn more about people like yourself. I wanted to see if I could gain insight on how to, I don't know, make his life better, maybe. Maybe even communicate with him on some level."

James pondered Pevnick's words for a moment. He stood and moved next to him at the window. In the fading light, seagulls flew in various formations, dipping into the ocean as if on cue, like patrons at a deli waiting for their number to be called. Glancing down, James noted a swarm of wood ants on the windowsill outside. They formed a distinct pattern that silently *told* him he was right; the notion that had eluded him earlier, when he and Etta were kissing, had been the answer all along.

Matching the doctor's quiet delivery, James spoke above a whisper, "Then you succeeded."

Pevnick looked at him, frowning. "What are you talking about?"

James returned his stare, then pointed outside. "You see those birds out there? How they form a distinctive pattern? And these ants, too, just outside the window?"

Pevnick squinted at the ants. "Yes," he said, hesitant but curious.

"They're talking to us. Or, I should say, *God* is talking to us."

"What are you saying, James?"

"As I said, you have to take a leap of faith. Will you agree that the Manti, my so-called *new* language, is valid, explainable, and usable?"

"Yes," said Pevnick, reluctantly. "Inasmuch as any made-up language can be. As far as I can tell, it has standard symbols that can be recognized by another person. With the training and repeated exposure, it could be learned and two people should be able to communicate with those symbols, like sign language, I suppose."

"Douglas was using the Manti, doctor," James continued. "I don't know how he learned it. Perhaps he has those extra sensory perceptions you've documented in some savants. But, the point is, he knows it and has written text on this notepad you left in his room and on the sheets from his bed…on anything he could get his hands on. All those scribbles you've found in his room were his attempts to tell us something. But, no one was listening…until now."

"Go on," said Pevnick, staring at the notepad. Even he could see, now, there were repeated patterns to the symbols he'd previously thought were merely doodles.

"I told you," James said, "I don't believe in coincidence. I think we were brought here so I could communicate with Douglas, so he can deliver this message to us."

Pevnick looked at James incredulously. "And who is sending the message, James?"

"You don't know, doctor? With all that is happening, you really don't know? Or, maybe you just don't want to believe…"

"Believe in what, James? Quit being so cagey."

"In *God*, Dr. Pevnick. God is sending this message."

"God?" said Pevnick, his face flushing with anger. "I told you, I don't believe in God."

"Then call him what you will: Jehovah, Yahweh, Allah, Mohamed, Buddha, the Great Spirit; it doesn't matter. There *is* a higher power. And it *is* directing us. You just don't see it."

"And you do?"

James rubbed his hand over his face before speaking, then turned and blasted Pevnick with anger, "Your view is limited, as it is with most *normal* people. Like so many others with your limited view, you think in terms of manipulation and machination over instinct and nature, greed instead of need, want instead of giving. Animals and nature have lived here for eons, evolved and survived, while we pathetic humans continue to destroy ourselves and the planet we live on. In truth, we all deserve to die. But, I'm afraid if that happens, we will irreparably tear the fabric of nature, itself, and upset a balance already in place and that we, in spite of all our flaws, are a part of. We must find a way to survive for the good of *everything*, if not *everyone*. We *have* to listen to this message."

Pevnick, shaking his head, queried through clenched teeth, "And what is the message, James?"

James looked at him as if he were talking to a child. "How to save the world. What else?"

CHAPTER TWENTY-TWO

Harvey Peet: Congenital Savant

Melbourne, Australia: Ten years ago

Harvey sat in a dark room in a corner of the massive building formerly and generically known as the "Orphan Asylum" in Melbourne, Australia. He was alone, as usual. People generally did not like to be around a kid whose head was the size of a melon and held eyes that scanned back and forth like the orbs of some alien robot. That, and he cussed so much that even street-smart orphans with their own ghetto language felt assaulted by his bursts of profanity. That was part of his "disease," his caretakers told the children. He was "severely retarded and had Tourette's syndrome," they said. It contributed to his almost constant grunting, sniffing, snorting, and the profanity. They "should just *ignore him*," was the advice.

But, Harvey did not want to be ignored. He knew he was different, but he had so much he wanted to share. By the time he was nine years old, he had read every book written by Herman Melville, Jules Verne, H.G. Wells, Jack London, Hemingway, Faulkner, Fitzgerald, Steinbeck, Leo Tolstoy, Ray Bradbury, Mary Shelley, Marjorie Kinnan Rawlings, as well as several versions of the Bible, the Torah, the Quran and many, many more books in every imaginable genre. He devoured medical textbooks and mechanical and science journals. He loved anything about anthropology, perhaps because he was trying to figure out exactly *what* he was. He wanted to tell people the details of these fascinating books and stories, but no one wanted to listen.

Harvey had become so isolated and ostracized by the other children, as well as by the caretakers, that eventually the decision was made to move him to some other place—at least during the day—where he could spout his gibberish and no one would mind. They took him to a nursing home for elderly people, most of whom had also been abandoned by their families. There, they believed he would find people who enjoyed listening to his shared stories, were patient with his speech and behavioral challenges, and appreciated the company. When he couldn't find anyone willing to listen, however, he took to meandering to the common room where they parked patients with dementia, and he would converse with them for hours, even if they were just staring at the wall, folded over in their wheelchairs, drooling on themselves. In fact, he seemed to seek these people out as they were the easiest to talk to and didn't seem to mind his "problems."

After several months, the driver who transported Harvey to and from the nursing home died in an automobile crash, and no one came to retrieve the troublesome boy. He didn't mind. By then, he had befriended a few of the nurses and had free run of the place for the next two years. The old folks were almost constantly dying off, and he would find an empty room and sleep there. The cafeteria served a buffet style meal, and he helped himself to it whenever he liked.

A kindly, old widow named Louise ran the cafeteria and felt sorry for Harvey. She made sure he got extra biscuits or pie or whatever treat she could find for him. He came to think of her as a sort of mother. He'd never known his parents, the couple who had abandoned him at the asylum after their family doctor had advised them that, "Harvey should be institutionalized as he will never be normal and, in all likelihood, will not live very long, anyway."

One day, he was in the cafeteria, waiting in line for food, when he saw a commotion unfolding in the back of the kitchen. He noticed several of the cooks and nursing staff looking at something on the floor, their hands clasped over their mouths, shaking their heads as if looking at a kitten that had been run over. Harvey, naturally curious, inched around the crowd to see what they were looking at and was surprised to find Louise lying on the floor, her usual ruddy cheeks pale; her lips blue. He pushed through the crowd of cafeteria workers, patients, and ill-trained staff, and felt her pulse. There wasn't one, and she wasn't breathing.

Harvey looked up at a nurse who was standing by, and said, "She's had a…a…damn, damn, he…heh…hell…*heart attack.* Go get the du…du…damn, damn, *doctor,* you twit!" The nurse blanched from his verbal assault, but ran off to find the facility's singular attending physician. Harvey began doing CPR, having read how to perform the procedure in one of the many medical texts he'd perused.

When the nurse could not find the doctor, she returned instead with other members of the staff and a medical crash cart. By then, Harvey was soaked with sweat from his resuscitation efforts, and panting and grunting more than ever. The nurses told him to back away, they would handle it now. Harvey did as he was told, but watched the nurses as they fumbled through the medical supplies and conversed about how to start the *defib-ree-ulator.* One of them kept trying to start an IV, but her inexperience crippled her and she kept missing the vein with the needle. They were taking *so long.*

His breathing recovered, Harvey grew anxious and impatient. Wordlessly, he managed to push past the fumbling nurses and grabbed the defibrillator. He ripped open Louise's dress—onlookers gasped—and told everyone to stay back as he charged the electric paddles of the machine. One of the nurses tried to stop him, so he held the paddles out in from of him, like shields, and told her to, "bu…bu…*back away.*" She did.

Harvey placed the paddles on Louise's chest. He watched the image on the screen; it showed a squiggly green line with fine bumps, which Harvey recognized as ventricular fibrillation—a severe, sometimes deadly rhythm, but one that could be reversed with an electrical shock. He recalled the initial jolt was supposed to be two hundred joules. He turned the switch on the machine to the mark that read "200," placed the paddles where they would deliver an electrical shock that would transverse Louse's heart (as indicated in the journals), and delivered the first defibrillation. When nothing happened, he turned the machine up to three hundred joules and delivered another one. This time, Louise's eyes opened wide, and she gasped.

"Ox...ox...y...gen," Harvey stammered. Now, the nurses seemed to be listening—they were certainly more cooperative. One of them put an oxygen mask on Louise, while another finally got an IV started. Then, they seemed unsure of what to do. One of them yelled, "Call an ambulance!" But Harvey knew Louise was not out of the woods, yet. He turned and dug through the medical supplies until he found a syringe filled with Lidocaine. He remembered it to be what the medical books called an *antiarrhythmic* drug used to stabilize a heart that has returned to function. He also remembered the dose (one milligram per kilogram) and, even as some of the nurses told him to stop—*he didn't know what he was doing!*—he drew up 70 milligrams and pushed it into the IV hub. Harvey told one of the nurses to follow up the Lidocaine bolus with a maintenance IV drip of one gram of Lidocaine to 250 milliliters of D5W. The nurse complied, and Louise stabilized.

The ambulance arrived along with the police. Several of the nurses talked to them, pointing at Harvey, and a policeman eventually approached. "You're going to have to come with me, young man," said the policeman. And so, Harvey was arrested for the first, but not the last, time in his life. He was eleven years old.

He was charged with loitering, as he was not supposed to be in the facility in the first place, and assault, which was downgraded to disturbing the peace. He was also initially charged with practicing medicine without a license, but that was downgraded as well, to "interfering with a medical professional" and, finally, thrown out after the judge reviewed what Harvey had done to save Louise's life.

Harvey was placed in a juvenile detention center where he was beat up almost every day. Sensing he would not last long in the hostile environment, he managed to check out every book he could on the subject of Aikido while on rare outings at the public library. Aikido is performed by blending one's movement with the motion of the attacker and redirecting the force of the attack, rather than opposing it head-on. This requires very little physical strength, perfect for Harvey as he was physically weaker than most boys his age. As he was attacked daily, he had an abundance of opportunities with which to hone his new skill and became so good he was eventually left alone.

After a few months, Louise recovered and found him at the detention center. She pleaded with the social director in charge of the center to let her take Harvey home. The director, by then frustrated and maddened by Harvey's daily barrage of insults and profanity, was all too ready to allow Harvey to leave.

At twelve years old, Harvey finally had a home and a family.

CHAPTER TWENTY-THREE

In New York, as in most of the eastern seaboard cities, those who had not begun to evacuate were either at stores trying to buy essentials for survival, or hesitantly going to work, hoping it was all a hoax, an exaggeration, or some sort of colossal mistake. But, for those who were not in a full blown panic, it was difficult to do anything, go anywhere, and find any semblance of normalcy.

Hordes of people, unsure whether to pick up and run, gather their loved ones, or just go to work, hovered like dementia patients, shuffling along sidewalks and locking on to any television set in public view that might give them some impetus to make a decision. Hundreds stood outside electronics stores, or sat drinking in sports bars, watching big screen televisions display minute by minute coverage of a nation succumbing to anarchy and fear.

"Good Morning America, if I can truly say that. I'm David Reynolds. My co-anchor, Debra Holstein, is out today," reported Reynolds, a noticeable look of worry on his face. His typically modeled hair was slightly askew, his impeccable suit appeared rumpled; his tie, loose.

"Reports coming in from analysts of the impending disaster— and let me add, there's still no agreement as to when it will happen— claim New York is most likely the worst place to be right now. Gas supplies ran out within hours of the Vice President's announcement yesterday morning, and highways and interstates are at a dead standstill. The National Guard has begun to respond, but there seems to be too few guardsmen to be effective in controlling the situation." Reynolds paused to take a breath, his typically stoic and unbiased expressions appearing unusually difficult to manage. "There are widespread reports of looting already," he continued, "and, while a press conference is scheduled for this morning, we still have not heard from President Cooper. Now, we turn to international field correspondent Stewart Cunningham in London, to hear what other countries are making of our dilemma and what, if anything, they plan to do to help. Stewart?"

The television images switched to a correspondent standing in front of Big Ben in London, his hair mussed from the wind as he held a microphone to his mouth. "Thank you, David," he began. "Just fifteen minutes ago, I spoke to Prime Minster Talbot, and he confirmed he has been talking with U.S. President Cooper throughout the night and has committed to send up to thirty thousand armed troops to the U.S. While he could not confirm details, Talbot stated the President has been talking to other world leaders who have offered assistance, including America's neighbors, the Canadian and Mexican governments, and that a massive, worldwide rescue and relief effort is under way. Here's a clip from that interview…"

Prime Minister Alfred Talbot, a distinguished looking man in his fifties, was standing in front of the Parliament building as the correspondent conducted the interview. The Prime Minister had been trying to reach his waiting car, but was stopped briefly to calm the barrage of reporters who'd approached.

"I've only a minute," said Talbot, "but, well, yes, the United States has historically been first in line when disaster struck in virtually every country in the world. They have been steadfast allies with England. Damn right we're going to help, and I hope every nation that has ever received help from the U.S. remembers we owe them… and it's time to repay that debt. Now, if you'll excuse me."

"Prime Minister," asked an off-screen reporter, "can you speak to the subject of political unrest that exists between the President and the Vice President?"

Talbot was almost in the door of his car when he twirled back to address the question. "Honestly, I can't," he answered. "It seems rather obvious the Vice President and the President are not on the same page, but I stand with President Cooper. He is a man I know and trust, and that's all there is to that."

Stewart Cunningham turned back to the cameras. "There you have it, David. So, it seems the U.S. does have assistance on the way. But the question is: Will help arrive in time? David?"

The scene returned to anchorman Reynolds as he continued his broadcast. "Thank you, Stewart, for that report. This just in, it has been confirmed that Canada has offered ten thousand troops, and they are already crossing the border into the New England area where President Cooper is believed to be…but, in the streets of New York, Baltimore, and Washington, D.C., the outlook is not as comforting as riots and looting continue…"

The scene changed again, and videos, many of which were being sent in by citizens with camera phones, showed total bedlam. People everywhere were fighting—individually and in crowds—stealing cars, and pushing postal workers out of their trucks. Windows were smashed, and screams and shouting filled the streets. The sounds of gunfire echoed between buildings and through alleys. Policemen tried to stop the chaos, but were quickly overcome by mobs of people. Tear gas floated through the air like a blistering fog. Fire fighters tried to push the crowds back with high-pressure hoses, and the mobs overcame them, too, pushing them to the ground and stealing their fire trucks as anarchy grew. Civility had become a luxury that'd dissipated like spilled alcohol.

***

Vice President Proger once again stood in front of a row of microphones, a cadre of reporters thronging the lawn in front of him. It was a bold move to stand in front of the White House—the President's official home—but, he had gotten word the President's family had been whisked away in the night. Besides, he'd had some of his own army move into D.C. to "help secure the growing unrest." People noted the new soldiers didn't wear traditional uniforms but, gripped by fear and anxiety, that was the least of their worries. Even the media didn't seem to notice or care about the origins of these troops, perhaps because the general thinking was that international troops were on their way to help, and these men must be part of the relief and rescue efforts.

This was Proger's attempt to spoil the broth a bit more, create enough doubt among the citizens to make them want a new leader, someone with a plan, someone who could save them. Still, Proger appeared nervous as he began his speech.

"These are troubling times," he began, a somber expression upon his face. "While we continue to await word from President Cooper, we've heard what you've heard; that he is holed up at a research facility, working with mentally challenged patients who are trying to come up with a recovery plan. I want to assure the American people that we, myself and other members of Congress, are doing everything we can to mitigate this disaster. People are evacuating, and we are aware of multitudes of traffic jams and fuel shortages. We ask you to be patient. State militias are moving into the most affected areas, and assistance will be forthcoming. You might have already seen these groups of soldiers—*our* soldiers— moving in, and I ask that you let them do what they are trained to do. I say again, if you are fifty miles or more inland, you should be safe from the tidal surge. If you live in areas outside of the projected target areas, please assist your fellow countrymen as they make their way out to you. Keep tuned to your televisions and radios for additional information.

"I will be leaving immediately for St. Louis to meet with members of the Senate and House to continue our mitigation and recovery plan. Please try not to panic. We are in this together, and we will help you. God bless and help us all."

Proger darted away before any of the news people could ask questions. He walked briskly out to a helicopter waiting for him on the lawn as the reporters first shouted after him, then looked confused and began to dissipate, their questions once again unanswered.

CHAPTER TWENTY-FOUR

The surface of the ocean bubbled, turning from turquoise to muddy brown, as six hundred feet below, a line of submarines steadily fired the specially-designed torpedoes into the crumbling continental shelf. Giant slabs of the underwater cliff fell away into the rise's own crevice that dug into the earth like a deep scar. The shelf slowly decreased in size, its mass grew smaller, foot by precious foot. Massive shock waves rocked the submarines and their crews, but they continued their seemingly endless task.

The water was so dense with rock, sand, and debris that operations were performed exclusively by sonar. Inside the SS Virginia, the crew was jostled back and forth like dolls tossed by an angry child. They were soaked with sweat, and most of them were scared witless. This was not a mission any of them had trained for, but they continued the job with intrepid doggedness. One of the seamen adjusted a picture of his girlfriend that had fallen onto his keyboard. The sub commander saw him and strode over. He could see the sailor was shaken.

"I…I'm sorry, sir. I know we're not supposed to keep personal items in the Ops room."

"S'okay," said the commander. "A submarine's got room for everything but mistakes. Let's not make any today."

The seaman nodded and went back to adjusting controls at his station.

The commander turned to his crew. "Keep at it, fellas. I think we're actually cutting that monster down to size! Navigation?"

Over the ship's comm system, a tinny voice came through, "Navigation, sir."

"Stay with the plan," said the commander, "but keep us back another five hundred yards. If we knock a big chunk off that thing, it could pull us down with it. Understand?"

"Understood, sir. The sonar, though, sir, is showing one of our fleet within one hundred yards of the precipice."

The commander frowned, looking into the sonar screen. "What the hell is he doing?"

"Looks like he's lining up for another shot, sir," answered the navigator, his voice edgy.

"Who is it?" the commander shouted, showing his agitation.

"Uh, this is Comm, sir," the intercom crackled. "It appears to be the Tennessee."

"Radio him, immediately. Tell him not to fire at that range!"

"Sir," the voice over the comm suddenly full of urgency, "I'm seeing their torpedoes are already in the tubes…wait…they pushed the launch!"

"Command to engineering, reverse!" the commander bellowed. "I repeat, reverse all engines, hard."

The SS Tennessee fired its torpedoes at the wall of the shelf, and the impact was immediate and catastrophic. A gigantic wall of rock collapsed, some of it sliding downward, while a massive part the size of Mount Rushmore toppled forward. The wall fell slowly at first, but quickly picked up momentum that stirred the sea and created a sucking vortex akin to an underwater tornado.

The Tennessee crew noticed their mistake, but it was too late. Even as their commander ordered a full reverse, the first "small" pieces of the wall—chunks as big as school buses—began raining down on the hull of the sub. Then, the rest of it came, like the giant hand of an angry God, and slammed down on the SS Tennessee, crushing it and pulling it into the bottomless crevice, as if it were nothing but a plastic, bathtub toy. As it descended, rapidly, its hull crushed, and explosions belched from the ship as air squeezed out. Within seconds, it spun out of sight.

The shock waves from the fallen wall and the destroyed sub rocked the crew of the Virginia as the ship bucked up and down, its metal exterior groaning with the added pressure and force. The ocean found every tiny crack in the hull and pushed its way in like a home invasion gang in the middle of a dark night. But, the crew stayed at their stations and went into immediate repair mode. Hydraulic gears shut down rooms where flooding threatened most. The quick reverse the commander had ordered before the blast helped pull the Virginia away from the same fate as the Tennessee.

The crew was awash in sweat and blood. A quick assessment revealed no one had been killed, but several critical wounds were reported, and the ship's med room filled quickly. The rest of the crew gathered their wits and returned to their stations, hearts and lungs pumping with fear and relief.

"Command to Navigation," said the commander. "You see anything?"

There was a moment of silence while the navigator searched the sonar screen, looking for something, anything, then he answered, his voice cracking, "No, sir. The Tennessee...she's gone, sir."

The commander looked around at his men. He knew he had to maintain morale any way he could. He summoned his own courage and addressed the ship. "Command to all stations. Give me damage reports and stay the course. We just saw what can happen if we get too close to that...thing. I'm not going to give you any BS, men. We might meet the same fate as the Tennessee. But, keep this in mind: we have a few million people on shore counting on us. If we go down, we need to make it count. No mistakes, gentlemen. Keep vigilant and, God willing, we might get out of this and save our country. That's what we're here for. Now, let's do our job."

It wasn't the Gettysburg Address, but the commander's words bolstered the crew. Those who could, returned to work with new zeal and cautious optimism. And all of them muttered a prayer to whatever God would listen.

CHAPTER TWENTY-FIVE

At the Beehive, Dr. Pevnick gathered his research group—James, Harvey, Jeremy, and Etta—and seated them in the study, across the table from President Cooper. James had his laptop open and chewed on his cheek excitedly. He and Etta exchanged furtive glances, but both knew the seriousness of the situation and tried to abate their growing interest in each other.

"Thank you for your time again, Mr. President," said Pevnick. "I know how busy you are right now, but James and, well, his think-tank here, want to present an idea to you."

President Cooper looked exhausted. Wearily, he said, "Okay. But, it will have to be brief. We've had submarines working all night, with some success. But we lost one, the Tennessee, about an hour ago. The Vice President has gone against me on my, excuse me, *our* plan, and he's persuaded more than half of Congress to side with him. He's also initiated an evacuation we were completely unprepared for, and the result has been utter chaos. In short, when I go on camera in…," he looked at his watch, "fifteen minutes, I have to convince the nation, perhaps the world, that I have not gone mad…nor abandoned them in their time of need."

James frowned at him. "You said you had 'some' success, Mr. President. What do you mean?"

"Well, the Navy tells me they think they've reduced the size of the shelf, perhaps as much as twenty to thirty percent."

James stared at the ceiling while he did some lightning

calculations, his fingertips tapping against his thumbs as he counted wordlessly. "If those numbers are correct, even the minimal twenty percent figure, you have already reduced the mass and so, the inertia and impact of the force..."

"In layman's terms, James...?" Cooper pleaded.

"You've already saved Florida and New York and all of the states north of Connecticut. In other words, millions of lives, sir."

Cooper looked stunned for a moment. He glanced around the table. Etta nodded and smiled, just a little. Jeremy gave a huge, toothy smile and snorted.

"Sounds about...*cuss*...*cuss*...right to me," said Harvey, grinning.

"That's wonderful news," said Cooper, genuinely pleased. "If we've done nothing else here, we can at least count that as a success. I pray I can count on your estimates. I have to tell America some positive news and explain why we've taken the direction we have."

"It's a relatively accurate estimate, sir," James assured, "if the Navy estimate of twenty percent is even close."

"Thank you, James. Now, I should be going...I have to coordinate the evacuation of those states still in harm's way. People will need time to prepare."

James looked at Dr. Pevnick as if willing him to say something.

"Er, uh, Mr. President," said Pevnick. "The group has a theory they need to talk to you about."

Cooper had stood, but paused. "Go ahead, be brief."

"All right," said James. "I've been evaluating our...situation as I've been trying to find other solutions. Analyzing the abilities of the submarines for our current objectives, we came across several pieces of news that Harvey thinks are related. You know, I don't believe in coincidences."

"Go on," said Cooper, perplexed.

James turned his laptop around so the President could see the screen. "You knew a man named Guy McAllister, didn't you, sir?"

"Yes, I know Guy. I haven't seen him in a couple years, since he retired from the CIA. Was a nautical specialist."

James showed him a picture of a burned shell of a car. "Harvey, would you explain your theory to the President?"

"Of course," said Harvey, suddenly animated. "I can't just sit here looking fabulous. Er, uh, McAllister was incinerated in a car explosion a few days ago."

Cooper frowned. "I'm sorry to hear that. I..."

James hit a few more keys on the laptop and produced another picture. This one showed a body lying on the front porch of a home with a blanket covering it and several policemen gathered around.

"Former Admiral Anthony Johnson," said Harvey. "Shot in the head when he went to get his mail, also just a few days ago."

Before Cooper could comment, James produced an Internet headline from a newspaper featuring a grainy picture of the outside of a bar in Maine, its windows spider webbed with bullet holes. He nodded to Harvey to continue.

"Several merchant seamen were gunned...damn, damn... *cuss*...down in a bar in Maine. It was reported yesterday."

Cooper looked to Pevnick as if wanting him to explain.

"Please listen to him, sir," said Pevnick. "This may be very important. At the very least, I think Homeland Security Director Finney should be made aware of these circumstances."

"Please, continue," said Cooper, sitting back down.

"A few years ago," said Harvey, "when McAllister retired from the CIA, he wrote a book about several nuclear devices the U.S. government had *misplaced* and offered some solutions to recovering them. One such device was the bomb off of ta...ta...*cuss*...Tybee Island, Georgia. In fact, at one point McAllister said he could, for the price of one million dollars, recover this device saying, in his own words: 'A small, private, but sophisticated submarine and a group of sailors, maybe five or six in number...'"

Cooper's mouth hung open as his astonishment grew.

"The seamen who were gunned down worked for a private submarine manufacturer in Maine, called Nemo Enterprises. Former Admiral Johnson had taken on contract work, as a private commander, also with Nemo. And this is what clinches it: McAllister was paid the sum of *one million dollars* as a contractor to Nemo."

"What are you saying, Harvey?" Cooper asked. "That these men are responsible for detonating the nuclear bomb off Cape Hatteras?"

"I cannot...*damn*...*cuss*...*cuss*...draw that conclusion from my evidence, nor is that my particular concern. My purpose for telling you this is to prove...*cuss*...there was a conspiracy, and that this device did not *accidently* move itself a few hundred miles to the north, then *accidently* detonate."

"What other proof do you have of a conspiracy?"

Harvey leaned forward and adjusted his smudged glasses. "Have you ever heard of a man named Aristotle Haufman?"

Cooper shook his head. "Not that I can recall."

"The Vice President has. In fact, one of Mr. Proger's oil companies, for which he served as a consultant and former chairman before being voted into office with you, issued a check in the amount of one million dollars to a shell company called Vestventures Incorporated, just a few weeks ago. Vestventures then hired a consultant, this Haufman character, who then funneled the money to Nemo in Maine and, bingo, McAllister ends up with a large deposit made to his bank account. You can guess how much. We, uh, kind of hacked into his account, sir. "

"One million dollars?" said Cooper.

"Correct!" said Harvey. "And here's another clincher: Haufman is the ad hoc General of a large contingent of militias throughout the Midwest. And, here's the best part..."

Harvey nodded to James to show the laptop again, so excited that he was squirming in his seat. James calmly turned the laptop around once more for Cooper to see. There was a picture of Vice President Proger and General Haufman, standing shoulder to shoulder, holding rifles proudly over the body of a slain buffalo. "Haufman and Proger are hunting buddies," said Harvey. "*Booyah!*"

Cooper rose angrily from his chair. He walked to the window in the room and looked outside, gripping his chin in thought. He watched as leagues of media people ran cables and set up satellite dishes, directed by the Secret Service, readying for the President's announcement. He closed his eyes; the muscle in his jaw flexed.

"One other thing, Mr. President," said James. "One of the seamen who were gunned down is still alive. Maybe your people should talk to him..."

"While they still can," added Harvey. "And, I hate to be insensitive, Mr. President, but I would suggest you have your former Chief of Staff Ken Fontana's body exhumed. It's entirely possible he was murdered."

Cooper turned back from the window, a stunned look on his

face. "What?"

Harvey shrugged. "A young man in prime cardiovascular health, and he drops dead from a heart attack? Combined with the other elements of the Vice President's betrayal, and this conspiracy to relocate and detonate the missing nuclear device, I think further investigation is warranted. Don't you?"

"I'll have Director Finney debrief all of you, immediately," the President said. "He'll need to know everything you told me." He looked around at the group. "Thank you...all of you. I know you've worked hard. Wish my own intelligence community worked as hard. Now, I have to go speak to the press. If you'll excuse me..."

James glared at Pevnick, prodding once again.

"There is one other thing, sir," said Pevnick.

Agitated and anxious from the news and the circumstances, Cooper was visibly impatient. "Quickly, please."

"James has something else to ask you. James?"

"Are you acquainted with the Starfire Project?"

Cooper hesitated, pondering the question, before answering. "I, just recently became aware of it. I met one of the scientists who worked on the project a few days ago, when we first became aware of the nuclear detonation and the fault line problem. Let's see, what was his name...?"

"Was it Carl Edwards?" asked James.

"Yes, I think that's right. Why do you ask?"

"I need to talk to him," said James.

"Of course. Arrange it with Director Finney. He'll be here shortly. Now, I really have to go. We'll talk more later."

"Good luck, sir," said Pevnick.

"Thanks, Stephen. I'll need it."

After Cooper left the room, Pevnick raised a question. "Why didn't you mention to the President why you want access to the Starfire Project, James?"

Etta had been silently observing the conversation. She straightened and cleared her throat.

"Be...cause," she began, hesitantly, almost startling the group, "because he could not handle the truth...right now."

"Do you think it will be any better later?" asked Pevnick, finding himself somewhat amused that Etta had spoken up on her own.

"Professor," she went on, "he just learned that the man he chose to be his second is, in fact, a traitor and conspirator. An enemy. Perhaps even a terrorist. We should not burden him with anymore right now."

Pevnick smiled benevolently at her. "I thought I was supposed to be the psych doctor here." He gave her shoulder a squeeze.

"Jeremy," said James. "How is your project coming?"

"My new toy? Ees Magnifique! Eet just needs zee power."

James nodded. "I'm working on that. I still need…a few more answers."

CHAPTER TWENTY-SIX

A dais and podium had been set up in front of the research facility, making it look like any other press conference that might occur in the Rose Garden at the White House. Only, this conference would be almost feverishly viewed by millions of people unsure if they'd be alive by the end of the week—perhaps the end of the day. They needed assurance that someone would save them, their loved ones, and their homes. President Cooper knew the gravity of his address as he stepped up to the row of microphones. Dr. Pevnick watched from the sidelines, wondering how the man would find the courage to do what needed to be done.

"I'm going to make a statement," the President began, "then I'll answer a few pertinent questions. I don't have time for soap opera innuendo or unsubstantiated inferences." Cooper paused, looking into each camera pointed at him.

"A few days ago, we learned of a catastrophic failure of the continental shelf off Cape Hatteras, North Carolina. As you are undoubtedly aware, a nuclear device was detonated, creating an unstable fault line. I now have reason to believe this device was set off intentionally and is possibly the result of a domestic terrorist scheme. We—myself, Homeland Security Director Finney and the appropriate departments under his direction, and those Congressmen who are loyal to America and able to discern right from wrong—will handle this crisis, along with the help of our armed forces. Even now, the Navy has a fleet of submarines performing mitigation efforts along the Carolina fault line. Unfortunately, one of those submarines has already made the ultimate sacrifice. God bless their souls. But, I promise, this country will be made safe. For the past forty-eight hours, I have been working diligently with the best minds in the world. We have made significant progress, and I can say, now, that many of the eastern seaboard states are no longer in peril. New York and most of New England are not in danger. Florida appears to be safe at this time, as well, and I am urging citizens in these states to remain home, and do not attempt to self-evacuate.

"That said," he continued, "at 3:00pm today, Eastern Standard Time, we will begin evacuating, to a safe distance of approximately fifty miles inland, the following states: Georgia, North and South Carolina, Virginia and the Washington, D.C., area, Delaware, Maryland, and New Jersey. This is a precaution only at this point. We will have fuel and food stores along designated evacuation routes. Temporary shelters will be established along the perimeter of the safe zone. Emergency funds will be available at these shelters. The National Guard and FEMA will be assisting this effort, along with some Army regulars. Our neighbors, Canada and Mexico, and partners from all across the world, the United Kingdom, France, Italy, and our allies in Eastern Europe are sending soldiers and assistance in an unprecedented relief effort. I am..."

Cooper paused, emotion creeping into his voice, and looked around at the army of multi-national reporters and cameras.

"I am overwhelmed by the positive response offered to the United States to assist with this disaster. And, I am humbled. But, I am also fortified and resilient that we stand together and be ever vigilant. *Together*, we will make it through this crisis. Now, I'll answer a few questions."

Pevnick watched his friend, the leader of the free world, and admired his strength. *There really are only a few people who can do the job of President,* he thought. *The man didn't even break a sweat.*

"Mr. President," called out one of the reporters, "why have you been hiding, and why did the *Vice* President announce this pending disaster and advise evacuation?"

Pevnick noticed the slightest twinge in the corner of Cooper's eye, a tiny flash of anger he quickly brought under control.

"The question about being 'in hiding' is one of those soap opera questions I warned you about. I have *not* been in hiding. I have worked non-stop, gathering *all* the information and formulating a plan *before* announcing we had a crisis. The Vice President did *not* act appropriately when I requested he handle a press conference for me while I addressed mitigation solutions. Nor did he act appropriately when he asked for my impeachment during one of the most challenging crises we have ever faced. If American citizens want me removed from office, then I will step down. But, while I am still President, I am going to do everything in my power to protect this great nation. As for the evacuation the Vice President called for, it has caused more problems than it has helped, and was, in many areas, not necessary. It was unplanned, and there have been numerous casualties and unparalleled chaos as a result, particularly in Florida and New York, where the evacuation, we now know, was not needed."

"Sounds like you're not on the same page with Vice President Proger," said another reporter.

"Same page?" said Cooper, almost growling. "We're not even reading the same book. That's all I'll say on that matter until this crisis is resolved."

Another reporter, one who was trying to make a name for himself by provocation, blurted: "Sir, you mentioned you were working with the best minds in the world. But, here you are, at a *mental research facility*, and it has been reported the people helping you are mentally retarded or somehow challenged."

"That's another soap opera question," said Cooper, embarrassing the reporter. "But, I'll answer, because I want the world to know who these people are. I have been working with scientists from all over the world, including Japan's Dr. Hisamoto and Austria's Dr. Heimel, as well as many of their colleagues. But, I have also requested the help of my friend and former advisor on national disaster planning, Dr. Stephen Pevnick. Dr. Pevnick introduced me to a special group of extraordinary people. Your choice of the word 'retarded' is as offensive as the 'N-word.' Please don't use it again to refer to these people instrumental in saving our lives. They don't think like us, it's true, and thank God for that! I, *we*, needed someone who could think outside the box and these people are doing it. If they have any 'challenges,' as you stated, they're the same ones Albert Einstein and Thomas Edison had."

As the embarrassed reporter sank into the crowd, his face red, another stepped up and asked, "Would it be possible to meet these people, sir?"

Cooper pondered the question for a moment and looked over to Pevnick, his eyebrows arched.

Pevnick shrugged his shoulders and nodded. He held up one finger indicating one minute and went inside to gather the savants. He emerged a few seconds later with the group tailing behind him. Etta tried to hide behind everyone, keeping her eyes to the ground. Jeremy looked around as if blinded by the attention, wearing pajama bottoms, a leather jacket and flip flops. Harvey smiled and waved as if he were running for President, himself, one shirttail tucked in, the other hanging out. James glanced at the crowd, but tried not to focus on anything, especially the grass in the lawn, as he feared he would count the blades. He squinted and looked up to avoid the crowd, already anticipating their questions and his answers, his shirt buttons mismatched to their holes and his zipper down.

Cooper waved them over. "This is Dr. Stephen Pevnick. Stephen?"

Pevnick approached the stand of microphones like a basket of snakes, looking hesitant, but assured. The group followed him, like baby ducklings behind their mother.

"Hu...Hello," said Pevnick. "Thank you, Mr. President. Uh, I'd like to introduce you to my...colleagues. But, first, I'd like to say this country could not have a better man to lead them, especially facing this crisis. President Cooper has worked around the clock for days without rest, and has made the best decisions possible based on the information available. You should trust him; you *can* trust him."

The crowd of reporters mumbled, generally, but there seemed a sense of acceptance, overall.

Cooper looked to Pevnick and nodded in appreciation.

"Now," Pevnick continued, "let me introduce to you my associates. Immediately to my left is Etta Kim, an engineer, specializing in oceanography. Next to her is Jeremy Clemens, a mechanical engineer and expert on time concepts..."

Etta kept her eyes on the ground, but gave an almost

imperceptible nod. Jeremy grinned broadly and took a bow. Harvey shook his head while James tried to keep his eyes averted.

"Next to Jeremy is Harvey Peet, a…brilliant researcher and historian."

Harvey winked at the crowd.

"And last, but not least, is James Tramwell, who many of you already know, I believe. He is our mathematical theorist and language expert. Would you like to say a few words, James?"

Surprised, James opened his eyes and glanced out over the heads of the sea of reporters. There were so many of them. Try as he might, he could not avoid counting; he counted their eyes, the buttons on their coats, the number who wore laced shoes versus those who did not. His eyes flashed around, back and forth, faster and faster, until his head began to swim and his vision blurred. Sweat poured down his face. He took a step and wobbled.

"James," said Pevnick. "Are you all right?" Then, he realized what was happening. He went to James's side, and whispered, "Close your eyes."

But it was too late. James had tried to count too many things and his brain had overloaded. His eyelids fluttered, and he fell to the ground, going into a full-blown seizure. Upset watching James suffer, Etta began to cry, her arms flailing around as she began stimming. Harvey and Jeremy just looked confused.

"'S'okay…s'okay…s'okay," repeated Jeremy, as if to assure himself.

"Damn, damn, sh…*cuss, cuss, cuss*," said Harvey, fighting the nervous tic that made him begin his cursing.

The crowd of reporters rushed forward. As Pevnick tried to help James, all tried to capture the scene on camera. Secret Service personnel pushed forward, as well, concerned the President might be at risk.

Cooper again leaned into the microphones. "This press conference is over," he stated. "Mr. Tramwell is obviously having a medical problem. We will keep you informed. Now, please take your exit."

Another reporter interjected, "But, Mr. President. These are the people you've trusted with the nation's security?"

One of the Secret Service agents pushed forward and shoved the reporter back. "The President of the United States has just issued an order. Now, move!"

Before the crowd could dissipate, James began to come to. He was talking, but incoherent. The reporter who was shoved away turned to his cameraman, and ordered, "Get this! Zoom in!"

James's eyelids flickered, and his eyes went wide, as if he were seeing something in front of his face no one else could see. "...it's not going...to work...the plan...not going to work. We need to...." The seizures started again, and he fell unconscious.

More Secret Service agents came from everywhere and managed to push back the eager reporters.

The savants helped Pevnick pick up James and carry him into the house. The moment that should have been a triumph, both for them and the President, faded into a gloomy melancholia for all of them.

***

In their hidden bunker in the otherwise quiet forest in Pennsylvania, Vice President Proger and General Haufman watched the telecast of the press conference. They glanced at each other, relieved, and smiled.

"That went better than I thought it would," said Haufman.

"I was worried for a little while," Proger admitted. "God, the man knows how to speak. But when he introduced those *retards*, well, the American people don't want to see something like that in times of a crisis. They want strength, not some lame effort led by a bunch of social rejects."

Proger stood up and shuffled to the lavatory to splash cold water on his face. Staring at his reflection in the mirror, he spoke to the general, "The public needs me. Let's proceed with the plan. Move in the militias...and the tanks. Start herding in motorists broken down along the roads, and show them we're here to help before the President can mobilize the regular Army. At best, it'll appear he reacted late. At worst, people will view him as weak... and impeachable; not fit to run this country."

"Yes, sir," said Haufman, standing erect and donning his new general's hat.

"One change, though, General."

"Sir?"

"Make that research center one of the first missions. I think we need to corral Cooper before he makes any more press statements."

CHAPTER TWENTY-SEVEN

James awoke with a groan, holding his aching head. He was surrounded by Dr. Pevnick, Mrs. Brown, the nurse, Magritte, and the rest of the savants. The President was still there, too.

"Looks like he's coming around," said Cooper. He glanced at the faces of the group. "What do you think he meant when he said, 'the plan wouldn't work?' Was he just delirious?"

"I'm...not sure, sir," said Pevnick. "He did have something else he wanted to discuss with you."

"Oh? Why didn't he?"

"I...I'm sorry, sir," said James, sitting up, rubbing his face. "You were in a hurry, but I have been going over my calculations and I'm not sure we'll be able to stop the fault line from getting worse."

"What? I just told the American people we were handling this. I gave them hope, son. Please don't tell me I have to take that back."

"I've gone over my figures and Etta has been helping me. She...I...*we* think that, even if we reduce the dimensions of the shelf, the fault line will still fail. Reports from the sub fleet state they have reduced the size of the shelf, but the fault line is still widening. We will have reduced the size of the resultant tidal wave, but there will still be a catastrophic failure, perhaps worse than we imagined."

Cooper shook his head. "It's too late for me to change our course of direction now..."

"I'm not asking you to. I...have another plan. It's risky, and we should still evacuate the coast in those areas we discussed previously, but I think, in the end, my plan could significantly deter the threat the fault line represents."

James turned to Etta. She smiled and took his hand. "Show him the model, Etta."

Etta picked up James's laptop, turned it on, and twirled the screen toward Cooper just as James began to explain.

"There is a field of frozen methane," he said, pointing with his index finger, "just to the west of the fault line area. If that field could be melted, or simply heated, the methane would thaw and erupt as a gigantic gas bubble."

"Like a big fart," said Harvey, grinning like a kid.

James frowned at him, then continued, "Many scientists believe this happens naturally and somewhat frequently in small amounts. But even small amounts are huge, and what many believe to be the cause of ships that disappear in the Bermuda Triangle."

Cooper's face went dead. It was as if all his faith, his belief that these people might be able to help, drained out of him like hope in a hurricane. "You mean the Devil's Triangle?" he said, glumly.

"Some call it that," said James. "Anyway, if we could time it right, if we had enough power to melt the field, whether instantly or near instantly, I think it could stop any wave action, perhaps even reset the fault line, if you will, back to a normal or near normal state."

Mechanically, Cooper said, "How could a field that large of any frozen matter be...*thawed*?"

James looked at the faces of his colleagues, as his own lit up with excitement. "With a laser."

Cooper took a deep breath, trying to remain calm and compassionate. In his heart, he knew this had been a hair-brained idea, but he'd been so desperate he had been willing to listen to anything, anybody who offered a solution. Now, he just felt empty.

"Well," he said. "I don't know about all the technology that's out there, but I know this from the old Star Wars defense program: there's not a laser in existence powerful enough to do what you're suggesting."

James nodded. "You're right." He stood up and approached President Cooper. "But, we're building one that should enable us to tap into an existing laser and intensify its effect. If we can direct the beam back through our atmosphere, then scatter the beam over a wide area, it could work. Harvey's read everything there is to know about it, theoretically. Etta's designed it, and Jeremy is building it. Almost finished; right, Jeremy?"

"*Oui*. Feen-ished, right. *Oui*," said Jeremy, calmly, talking like he had just finished replacing a flat tire on a car.

"You're telling me," said Cooper, "the four of you have built this device here in the backyard, while doing all the research on evacuation demographics, fault line restructuring, and uncovering a conspiracy against the nation, all in the past couple of *days*? How could you possibly have done that?" His tone was not merely one of a non-believer, but one who harbored more than a little anger.

"We...had help," said James.

"From who?" Cooper demanded.

The group all looked at each other, but said nothing.

Finally, Pevnick spoke up. "My son, sir. Douglas. He helped them."

Cooper looked confused. "Your son, Stephen? I thought your son was dead."

Pevnick nodded. "That's what I've told people for years. He was hurt...his brain damaged beyond any hope of recovery. But James has found a way of communicating with him, and..."

James interrupted, "Or, he's found a way to communicate with us. He's using a system I thought I had created. A language, if you will, I thought was derived from symbols I see in my head that I've recorded. Now, I find it came from actual patterns...from nature. And they are telling us everything we need to know. Douglas has been writing in this language—we're not sure how he knows it—but it is as clear to me as English is to you. His writings have assured me we must take a different tactic."

Cooper shook his head in disbelief, his tolerance and faith in the group all but diminished.

"I...can't believe this. I'm disappointed you weren't more candid with me, Stephen. This sounds so, well, I don't want to insult any of you, but it sounds like the plot to some silly sci-fi movie. Super-powered lasers, the Devil's Triangle; I can't go along with this. They'd lock me up and throw away the key. What we have been doing is unconventional enough, and I've trusted you knew what you were doing. But, this is too much. I can't believe in this, in you, anymore. I put the lives of millions of innocent people at risk. I'm sorry. This stops here."

Cooper began to leave, but James shot up and darted in front of him.

"Please, sir," he begged. "Listen. We don't want millions of people to die, either. That's why we are suggesting this plan."

"I'm sorry, James," said Cooper. "But, try to see it from my point of view. It's fantastical, unbelievable to begin with, then you tell me you learned this from a brain-damaged patient my *friend* and *advisor* has been telling me was dead for years? I'm sorry. I have to go."

"Wait, sir. Please," James pleaded on. "Answer one question: Do you believe in God?"

Cooper hesitated before answering. "Yes, son. I do. More than anything. My faith has kept me going so many times… It's the one thing I've always been able to believe in."

"Then believe in Him one more time, Mr. President. Because God is telling us what to do, how to save ourselves; we're just not listening. Let me show you. Dr. Pevnick, do you have that notepad, the one Douglas was writing on?"

"Yes," said Pevnick. Reluctantly, he handed it to James.

James took the pad to the window. "Mr. President, would you please come look at this?"

Cooper complied, slowly approaching the window, wondering what he was going to see. There was a flock of birds moving in a pattern. The wind blew, and the long grass shifted in swirling patterns.

"Do you see those patterns, sir?" he pointed. "That one, there, with the birds? Now, look at this page. Do you see the similarity? And there, see the grass moving, changing, but coming back to the same pattern?"

"Yes. I suppose I do." Cooper began to think of the past few days, recalling his own observation of nature and its patterns. *Could it be?* He wondered skeptically. When he'd run for the office he now held, he asked people to believe in him. People who were diametrically opposed to some of his views. Now, he wondered, could he do the same?

"Good," said James, excited. "Finally, look at these other patterns

Douglas has written down. These patterns are what I've used in making my language, something I've been calling *Manti*. Each one says something, or I should say it *means* something or elicits a certain knowledge—a readable knowledge, if you can interpret the symbols. For instance," he pointed, "this one means *sea* or *ocean*. This one means *sky* or *space*. This one is *conflict, war* or *fight*. This one, *power* or *strength*. This is *heal* or *mend*. This is *ice*. This is *star*. There are hundreds of these symbols. They are repeatable as necessary with any language. But, they are also present in nature. And if you can believe this is a language, you have to believe that someone, or some*thing*, is trying to give us a message." He paused, waiting for the President to comment. When he didn't, James added, "You know I don't believe in coincidences."

"So, you're saying…"

"Yes, I'm saying God is telling us how to save ourselves. He has been all along. We just haven't been listening."

"And what is *He* telling you, or us?"

"Do you remember when I asked you about the Starfire Project?"

"Yes?"

"Well, the Starfire Project uses a laser system, and a newer science called 'adaptive optics' to magnify images of the light a star produces in order to give us a better picture of the star, itself. We are able to see farther and more clearly into space than ever before. Follow?"

"Go on."

"A laser consists of a gain medium inside an optical cavity. If we can energize that medium, the power of the laser would be strengthened exponentially. It's called *pumping* the laser. If we can reverse the Starfire system to target earth, combine it with *our* power source, which will be a combination of a solid state and concentrated free electron laser, then direct that super-powered laser into the ocean where the methane field is, it should melt the field, like an enormous microwave, and cause a giant burp, if you will. Which will, hopefully, realign the fault."

By the time he stopped talking, James was vibrating with energy and passion.

"What about the ocean?" Cooper asked. "Won't the heat kill all the marine life, or warm the ocean and cause another catastrophe even more harmful down the road?"

"No," James answered confidently. "The laser will only affect that solid on which it lands. It should pass through the sea as though the sea wasn't even there. The methane eruptions might kill *some* sea life, but it won't permanently harm the ocean. Right, Etta?"

Etta nodded vigorously. President Cooper fell silent, trying to digest the new information and weigh it with his own religious beliefs.

"You know," he said, finally, "even if you could convince me, there is no way I could tell the American people this."

Pevnick stood up. "Who says you have to? Sir, until last night, I thought my son was a brain dead vegetable, to be perfectly frank. Today, I'm beginning to believe in *something*. If not God, then at least something more powerful than all of what we know. Working with this group the past few days has opened my eyes, made me believe that science and cold facts are not the only things that represent truth. Somewhere along the line that is our lives, there is another part of the equation we can't explain. Call it faith, God, Allah, or, like James said, the Great Spirit, if you will. Whatever it's called, it is inexplicable and wonderful at the same time. You and I both know, even if we can begin this evacuation, there will be mass chaos, looting, panic—all worse than things are now. We still won't really know if we've evacuated everyone as far inland as we should. The Vice President seems to be mounting an offensive created to spread civil unrest. The sooner we can intervene with some…I don't know…" Pevnick drifted off, searching for the right words. "We need a miracle," he finally said, "and I've never been one to believe in them. But these people, James, Etta, Harvey, Jeremy… they've ignited something in me. I…I don't even know what I'm saying anymore…I'm sorry."

The professor was fatigued and had become emotional, to his own surprise. His eyes filled with tears, and he had to stop talking. "I…have to go check on my son. He…might be trying to tell me something." He walked away, sniffling and taking the hearts of everyone in the room with him.

"Wait, Stephen," said Cooper. "I'll go with you." He turned to James. "James, I'm going to pray, too. Maybe I'll get some answers. Maybe, like you said, the solution's there, if we're willing to listen.

Director Finney is outside. Tell him you need to talk to Carl Edwards about Starfire. Tell him *I* want you to talk to him. But, whatever you do, don't tell Finney why. He's too practical; he'll never believe it, and he won't help you if he thinks you're crazy. Then, tell Dr. Edwards *I* need to talk to him." He turned to leave, then pivoted and said one last thing, "And, keep this in mind: we do no harm. If you can stop or alter this crisis in a way that doesn't endanger lives, let's proceed."

Cooper left the room.

James gazed around at his friends, grinning from ear to ear. "This is going to be fun!"

CHAPTER TWENTY-EIGHT

Magritte and Mrs. Brown huddled in the kitchen, worrying about James, as well as Douglas Pevnick. Sipping coffee, they tried to console each other as the television played back the scene from the press conference. A shaky image showed James coming out of the seizure, spittle dripping from his mouth as he muttered what sounded like incoherent babbling. Mrs. Brown and Magritte knew now, it hadn't been babbling.

A pretty blonde anchorwoman shared her take on it. "There you have it," she said, looking into the camera, "just a short while ago, President Cooper finally addressed the nation. And, while his comments tried to add stability and offer explanation to the current crisis facing America, what you just saw only invited more questions: Who are these people the President has chosen to guide the nation's mitigation efforts? What are their qualifications? How did this rift between the President and Vice President happen? Who is right? And, will we figure it out in time to save the threatened east coast and the millions who live there?"

She paused briefly before moving on to another topic. "In a related story, we talked with Homeland Security Director Alan Finney this morning, minutes before he was whisked off to join the President at the private research facility owned and operated by Dr. Stephen Pevnick, a former advisor to the President on national disaster planning."

The image on the screen changed to an earlier recorded

interview that began with a microphone being stuck in Director Finney's face. He looked none too pleased to answer questions, but stopped to make a comment.

"Look," said Finney, his eyes focused on the off-camera reporter holding the microphone, "I'm not at liberty to discuss the nation's security, but I can tell you this: I've been coordinating with various government agencies from every country you can imagine, along with our National Guard, FEMA, The Red Cross, and stateside armed forces. We *will* be prepared to assist in evacuating people and establish recovery projects in every affected area. As for whom we should be listening to for direction, President Cooper is *still* the President of this nation. I know him not only as an outstanding leader, but as a trusted friend. I would…no, I *am* trusting him with my life and the lives of my family. You should, too."

***

Hordes of tanks, armed personnel carriers, and the rag tag militia soldiers charged forward through the countryside of Maine, dust and debris churning behind them like the wake from a battleship. They crunched through growing fields with no regard for the acres of produce they destroyed or fences they knocked down. Angry farmers confronted them, but were pushed aside or threatened with incarceration. If they emerged from their homes armed, they were surrounded and their firearms taken away. The militia plodded ahead, fueled by its singular mission to dominate and control their assigned areas. Prisoners, including several National Guardsmen who tried to stop the marauders were taken, bound and bloodied, and shoved into the backs of covered trucks.

One field commander, a brash, hardened redneck, used a satellite phone to make a call to his leader. "General Haufman," the officer greeted his superior. "New Dawn One field report."

"Go ahead, Commander," said Haufman.

"We are approaching the target, sir, about a half hour out." He looked out toward the ocean, catching glimpses through the heavy forests along the coast of Maine, surprised at how easy their campaign was going. "We've encountered very little resistance, only one small band of Guardsmen we took prisoner."

Haufman was pleased. The prisoners would be beneficial to them. If the enemy could scramble their jets, they would never fire on U.S. citizens.

"Very good, Commander. You shouldn't have a problem at the research center. There are only about fifty Secret Service agents with the President. Your mission is to capture the President. Let nothing stand in your way. Understood?"

"Roger that, sir," said the field commander, excited his group would have the honor of apprehending the President. History was about to be made, and he would be a part of it.

***

James was video conferencing with Dr. Carl Edwards of the Starfire Project. Director Finney sat in to assess the conversation and the direction of the "New Plan." He was a smart, hard-charging manager of the premiere security force of America, but he found it extremely difficult to follow conversations among scientists.

"What you're suggesting has never been done, Mr. Tramwell," Dr. Edwards said from his laboratory, his eyes looking preternaturally huge behind his thick glasses. "Actually, we've never even thought to try. But, I suppose, based on your figures, it could be done. I'm going to need additional data from you, the total power impact of your...device. I'll also need coordinates of the methane field, at least a ballpark estimate."

Having anticipated this question, James leaned forward and rested his arms on the conference table. "That's coming to you as we speak. But, I have to be honest, we haven't fully tested the device, so we're a little unsure on the total power factor. We think we're working with solid theory here...but, until we actually *do* it, some of this will be best guesstimate."

Edwards looked perplexed. "Okay... Are you sure this is all right with everyone involved? I mean, we're talking about my baby here, and my baby costs taxpayers about ten billion dollars."

"The President called you, didn't he, Dr. Edwards?" Finney asked.

"Uh, yes, sir," the scientist replied, visibly uncomfortable. "But, I don't know if he knows the science of all this. And, frankly, if it doesn't work, or even if it *does*, I'm not sure a laser, even one this powerful, could melt a field of frozen methane that's hundreds of square miles across. I mean, there are so many factors: how deep is the field; will it ignite rather than just melt…"

"Dr. Edwards," Finney interrupted, "while we appreciate your concern, your President has given you an order during a national crisis. We don't question that. Understood?"

"Well, sure. After all, you're footing the bill." He threw up his hands, then removed his glasses and wiped the lenses with the edge of his lab coat. Without the glasses, his eyes looked unnaturally small. "I'm just asking you, begging you…please don't break my toy."

"I won't," said James, grinning. "Who knows, maybe it'll work better when we're finished."

"Haardy-har-har," said Edwards, childishly. "Let me know when you're ready, and we'll flick the switch. Mr. Finney, you'd better make sure the Navy has moved out of the area."

"They were ordered out over an hour ago. I'll check their progress," said Finney. He dialed a number on a sat phone he pulled from his coat pocket. "This is Finney to Underwater Command. Confirm you're clear."

A tinny voice, the commander of the SS Virginia, answered back, "We're clear, sir. None too soon, if you ask me. We knocked down a good part of that shelf, but the more we knocked it down, the more the fault line grew. It was like the weight of the debris was pushing it open. We started getting so many tremors, we thought the ship would shake apart."

"It's not over, yet," said Finney. "Just put a safe margin between you and that area. We'll let you know if you have to go back in. And, Captain?"

"Yes, sir?"

"Thank you for what you've done. We won't forget the sacrifice the Tennessee made. Hold on to your horses, and Godspeed."

"We're tight and right, sir."

CHAPTER TWENTY-NINE

President Cooper entered an upstairs room to find Dr. Pevnick kneeling by the bed of his son, holding his hand. Douglas was not looking well. He was comatose, sweating, breathing shallow, and pale.

"Why did you let everyone believe Douglas was dead, Stephen?" the President asked.

Pevnick turned his head to gaze up at his friend. "I don't have a good answer for that, especially now. Maybe I didn't want people to know, as one of the leading specialists in brain function and behavioral science, I was a flop who couldn't help his own son. That, and in spite of all my training and experience, I could only believe what I could see." The scientist returned his attention to Douglas while he continued to speak to Cooper. "His EEG showed little evidence of brain activity, the conventional tests we've used for decades to determine life. Today, I'm not so sure that is truly our best gauge, or if we know even half as much as we think we do. The ability he has shown to communicate is, well..."

"A miracle?"

Pevnick nodded, then bowed as he reached up to wipe a tear. "I've wasted so much time..."

Cooper knelt next to Pevnick, and wrapped a comforting arm around his friend. "Let's pray, Stephen. For Douglas. For everyone."

They began to pray.

***

Outside, at the edge of the grounds to the Beehive, militia forces appeared, dark and deadly, from the tree line. The field commander in the lead armed personnel carrier stopped abruptly, stepped from the vehicle, and pulled a radio mike out of the cab.

"New Dawn Command to all units," he said with calm authority. "We'll split right up the middle here, and flank to either side. Let's move, soldiers!"

XM8 tanks and Stryker units armed with 12.7 millimeter machine guns and 40 millimeter grenade launchers divided to each side, like Moses parting the ocean, and rumbled through the long grass, spreading across the acreage like an unstoppable plague.

***

As the submarine fleet moved away from the fault, the line began to fail. Its cavernous maw opened, and the teetering shelf at its edge fell away, pushing an underwater wall of water toward the coast. Inside the SS Virginia, the crew watched helplessly as the ocean floor deteriorated and created the tsunami. To the onlookers, watching on video screens fed by remote cameras, the scene was like watching the end of the world and they were on the precipice. They'd be the first to see it fail and the first to go with it. Every seaman on theirs, and every other ship, couldn't help but hold their breath. Watching the turbulences coming their way on the sonar screens was like watching the shockwaves from a nuclear blast.

"Get the Homeland Security Director on the phone," said the Virginia's captain. "This is not good, gentlemen."

***

The savants were gathered in the workshop, along with Finney, when he got the call. Jeremy was just finishing up last-minute adjustments on his toy, a car-sized piece of sophisticated machinery, with wheels, blinking lights, tubes, and wires that emitted more noises than a video game arcade.

Finney hung up his phone, sweat collecting along his brow. "It's not good, people. Underwater Command has reported the fault line opened up. The shelf…has collapsed. Our evacuation plan is going to be too late!"

"Then we have no time to lose," said James. "Jeremy, are we ready?"

"*Are we ready?*" Jeremy mimicked. "Are we ready? Do we have zee power?"

"Yes," James answered, "the Army Corps of Engineers set up the solar panels for us. At least some of them. Let's hope it's enough. You ready to hook up?"

"*Oui.* Hook up. Ha! *Oui.*"

"Let's do it, then," said James.

The group wheeled the laser to the doors and out of the workshop. Scattered throughout the tall grass of the adjacent acreage were dozens of solar panels, huge cables the size of a man's arm snaked out from them and up to the workshop. Jeremy picked up one of the cables and connected it to his machine. Everyone put on sunglasses as Jeremy hit the switch. The machine fell silent, then began to hum and crackle.

James grabbed his phone and called Dr. Edwards. "We're ready, sir. We don't have tracking ability, so we're going to fire the laser. You'll have to pick up the beam and allow the Starfire scope to absorb it and re-direct. Got it?"

"Yes," he answered, after taking in a deep breath. "I'm ready."

Jeremy flicked another switch and a blinding light enveloped the group as a beam shot from the machine and into the atmosphere.

Dr. Edwards and a group of assistants in his lab watched the wall of monitors that showed the Starfire Telescope in space. They could see the laser beam punching through the dark sky like a beacon.

"Here goes," said Edwards, turning knobs to maneuver the telescope.

The orbiting Starfire began to turn and move forward. Slowly, it moved in the direction of the laser beam, and finally into its path, then absorbed the intense light until the scope, itself, was glowing impossibly bright. Turning again, it slowly re-directed the light back toward Earth, the beam finer but more intense, glowing blue-white, like the sun.

The beam sliced down through the sea, where it lit up the ocean floor. A green glow began to spread. Small bubbles initially seeped through fissures, then grew larger. At first the bubbles were the size of golf balls, then grew to the size of footballs, then small cars, shimmering like an enormous curtain of diamonds. Then, a huge rumble sent shockwaves through the water as a giant, singular, gas bubble spewed up from the ocean bottom. Then another. The bubbles, the size of football stadiums and larger, belched from the depths, uniting and expanding as they ascended, growing ever larger.

The captain of the SS Virginia watched through the sub's periscope as the bubbles lifted, creating a forcible suction as they did. He called Finney, and reported, "Sir, we are seeing the bubbles, if you can call them that. But, it doesn't seem to be doing anything, the fault is still opening. The first tsunami just passed us."

Finney had his phone on speaker, and everyone heard the message.

"That's what I was afraid of," said James. "The beam is not widespread enough."

"Great," said Finney, sarcastically. "I'll go tell the President…"

"No, wait," said James. "I've got another idea. Or, I should say, Douglas had this idea."

He opened his notebook and looked at the strange symbols again, confirming his idea. He showed it to Finney. "I don't expect you to understand this, but this symbol here means 'sun.' But, the one next to it means 'distribute' or 'spread out.' And this one means 'satellite' or 'moon,' which is a satellite. I think Douglas was trying to tell us to use a satellite system to distribute the beam."

Finney looked at James as if he were a madman. "You're right, I don't have a clue what you're talking about. But, the President seems to trust you and we don't have many options. If you think it might work, just do it. And, son, you need to hurry."

James grabbed his phone again. "Dr. Edwards, we're not getting the intensity we need. From where you're at, can you track the old Vela Project with your satellites?"

"The old nuclear detection system?" asked Edwards, confused.

"Yes," said James, his voice unusually urgent.

"Sure, we have to navigate around it sometimes. Why?"

"We need to use it to disburse the beam more; make it wider."

"Uh, how's that?" asked Edwards, shaking his head.

"I want you to redirect the Starfire's beam away from the ocean and aim it at the Vela satellite."

"And…what will that do?"

"I'm hoping the bhangmeters, the photo sensors that detect the light from Earth, can act as mirrors, deflect the beam back to Earth and scatter it over a wider area, like a…a shotgun."

Edwards punched in data on his control board. "It might be worth a try, James, but we'll need to redirect the Vela, and I'm not sure we can do it from here."

"You have to try, Dr. Edwards," James pleaded. "The fault line is deteriorating quickly, and the shelf has already failed. There will be a massive tidal wave hitting the eastern seaboard in just over an hour, unless we can stop it."

"O…Okay," said Edwards. "We can try, but I'm going to need permissions from—"

Finney grabbed the phone from James. "Dr. Edwards, this is Homeland Security Director Finney. You have my authorization to do whatever it is you have to do. This is absolute priority. There are no alternative strategies at this point. Do you understand?"

"Yes, sir. Right away, sir."

Finney handed the phone back to James. "Do what you can, son. I'm going to go tell the President. God help us all."

A crackle came across Finney's radio earpiece, followed by an excited voice. It was one of the Secret Service agents standing guard outside. "Sir, we are being flanked by a group of hostile militia."

Finney ran to the window. Within a rising cloud of dust, he could make out tanks and personnel carriers surrounding the compound. "What the…?" he muttered, imagining the approaching army as what the Battle of '73 Easting must've looked like in the first Gulf War. He pushed the transmit button on his radio. "Agent, the President is still inside this building. Rally your men, and tell them I want the residence surrounded and protected at all costs. That means getting the big guns out of the trucks. And call in reinforcements. This is not a drill. I'm calling the Chairman of the JCS and have him order in air support. You got that?"

Finney ran out of the workshop, leaving the savants behind, and headed toward the house where the President conferred with

Professor Pevnick. As director of the nation's security, and having envisioned every possible disaster that might fall upon the country, he had never in his wildest dreams thought of this one. He glanced at the advancing militia as he ran, still in disbelief that someone would launch a coup while the country was on the verge of disaster. But, even as the thought occurred to him, he started to think it was not a coincidence.

Off the eastern coast, a few hundred miles south of the research facility and another hundred miles out to sea, an enormous swell began to emerge on the surface of the ocean. It was almost seven hundred miles long and picking up pace as it grew.

Finney barged into the house and found his way to Douglas Pevnick's room. Upon entering, he discovered President Cooper and Dr. Pevnick kneeling by Douglas's bed.

"Uh, I'm sorry to interrupt, Mr. President," Finney said, his face flushed and sweaty, "but this is very important."

"What is it, Alan?" asked Cooper. "Dr. Pevnick's son is, well, he's not doing well..."

"Sir, the compound is surrounded by unauthorized militia, armed with tanks and heavy artillery. To make things worse, sir, the laser beam wasn't strong enough to thaw more than a small section of the methane field. The fault line breached, and a tidal wave was produced. James is working with the Starfire team, but it doesn't look good. They think the wave will hit the coast in about an hour."

The look on Cooper's face was initially one of shock, then his jaws clenched. "I...let the people down. We...should have evacuated earlier. Go ahead and alert all Emergency Operations centers and have them do an immediate evacuation. I'll look like an idiot, but if it saves a few lives, we have to issue that order."

"Agreed, sir," responded Finney, "but we'll have to do it on the run. Maybe James and his brainy pals can do something, but I've got to get you out of here, keep you safe."

Cooper shook his head. "You want to keep me safe, Alan? Then give me a damn gun. Let's see what this militia is made of."

"Sir, I can't do that. My job is—"

"*My* job is to keep America safe," the President interrupted, "and your job is to help me do my job. Granted, I might not have done it very well, recently, but... Look, it's possible none of us will be here tomorrow. If I'm going to go, I'm taking out some of the people who created this problem. Understood?"

Finney nodded. He really liked this president. "Yes, sir!"

James was still on the phone with Edwards when he first heard the approaching militia. He looked out the window of the workshop and saw the approaching tanks. *Not now!* He thought. Then, an idea came to him. "Dr. Edwards?"

"Yes, James?"

"Have you taken control of the Vela satellites, yet?"

"We think so. We're trying to manipulate the bhangmeter panels now, but the technology is old; it's required several different configurations from our computers."

"Just get them close, Dr. Edwards," James said calmly. "This isn't brain surgery. Let's just try not to incinerate Charleston, okay?"

Edwards shook his head at James's nonchalance, but said, "Okay, if you just want close…"

Harvey was standing by, but did not share the same calm demeanor as James. "Fu…fu…*cuss, cuss, cuss*! Fire those damn things!"

James looked at Harvey, and curiously raised his eyebrow.

Harvey shrugged and grinned. "At least I didn't use profanity."

CHAPTER THIRTY

In the Starfire Project control room, last second adjustments were made. This was unprecedented territory, and everyone was nervous. The smallest mistake could make things even worse than they already were.

"Let's try this again," said Edwards, under his breath.

A camera from another satellite allowed the Edward's project team to watch on a large Hi-Def screen as the Starfire Laser moved and aligned with the numerous satellites that made up the antiquated Vela Project nuclear detection system. The Starfire began to glow, again, and the heavens lit up like a nova for an instant. The beam shot out and struck the Vela satellites, then splintered into dozens of beams that arced toward Earth and stabbed into the ocean like meteorites.

The newly super-powered beams punched into the ocean, piercing its depth like a warm knife through soft butter. They found their targets on the bottom and, even from the incredible depth, the red, volcano-like glow was detectable from the satellite video feed. The seafloor began to vibrate, then crack. Methane bubbles emerged through every new fissure. The bubbles began to clump together as they rose to the surface, quickly forming into one massive bubble, dozens of miles wide. As it increased in size and velocity, the tidal wave rolled toward it.

The two forces of nature collided in a thunderous impact. Water sprayed hundreds of feet into the air, creating an enormous vortex, a man-made tornado that whirled for a moment, then splashed back into the sea, creating smaller, harmless waves that within moments subsided as the sea regained its calm.

The ocean bottom shifted under the enormous weight and movement, as if it were being pressed by a giant iron that smoothed out its wrinkles and returned it to a peaceful mesa. The fault line realigned and settled into itself, just a harmless, though uneven, crack in the ocean floor.

Instruments tracking the now-vanished tidal wave showed nothing but calm as the ever-present currents of the sea momentarily stopped, as if not knowing which way to go.

In New Mexico, the Starfire Project team jumped up and down like kids getting ice cream as reports from oceanographers and meteorologists began pouring in. Then came the barrage of media reports—from every civilized and scientific nation—all sharing the same message with only slight variations: the tidal wave had subsided and the sea had regained its relative calm.

A message from the SS Virginia came over the speakers in the Starfire room, as well as James's cell phone outside the lab: "SS Virginia to Landside Operations," the captain's voice began, "I'm not sure what you guys did, but that was some of the best fireworks we've ever seen. We were rocking and rolling for a while, but we're all good now. Sonar shows everything is normal. Incredible job, men!"

The savants heard the message and everyone turned to smile at Etta, acknowledging the captain's oversight. But their happiness was short-lived as they heard the tanks roll in. A loud explosion rocked the workshop as a shell hit the bank of solar panels, destroying more than half of them. The beam from the Starfire Laser faltered, then blinked out.

The voice of Dr. Edwards erupted from the speakerphone, "James, what happened? We just got a power surge and you went offline. We were going to shut down the beam, but it seems to have shut itself down."

"Uh," James stalled, searching for the right reply, "we're being attacked by a renegade militia. They fired a missile into our power source."

"What?"

172

The advancing army was almost on top of them as Finney and Cooper, along with a phalanx of Secret Service agents, stormed toward the workshop, guns drawn.

"Everyone inside and stay away from the windows," Finney commanded. "We'll make a stand from here."

"Where is Professor Pevnick?" asked Etta, her face a mask of concern.

Cooper addressed her question with as much compassion as he could, "He's inside with his son. Douglas is not doing well, and he wanted to stay with him."

The Secret Service agents took their places alongside the window, and began prepping their weapons. Some errant shots rang out from the field and found their way to the workshop, punching holes in its old wooden sides.

"Mr. President," said Finney. "I've called in the airstrike, but it may take a few minutes for them to get scrambled. We still have time to get you out of here."

Cooper looked at him sternly. "Not a chance. I want to make a stand. This mess will obviously end up in court and spawn congressional hearings and investigative committees for years. But, today, I have the opportunity to put a bullet through the heads of those turncoats who started this war, and that's a chance I'm not going to miss." He looked at the savants, all of whom were standing wide-eyed, surprised at his comments. "Sorry, young people, but that's the way I feel."

"Um, Mr. President," James said awkwardly, "in case you didn't hear, sir, our plan worked. The sea and the east coast are now safe."

Cooper looked around at their faces and smiled, though his eyes were wet. "Splendid, James, and all of you. You helped make our nation safe. I, we, won't forget your help."

Suddenly, machine gunfire ripped through the walls of the workshop, sending splinters and dust through the air. There were loud *thwumps* as tanks fired their rounds, and the walls of the workshop began to fall. The ground shook, and more bullets zipped past the group as they scrambled, looking for a safe place to shield themselves.

Finney took a hit in the shoulder that spun him around before dumping him on the ground. "Damn," he cried, clutching his bleeding arm. "Everyone take cover!"

The savants hit the ground as the Secret Service agents fired back at the attacking militia, then used themselves as shields for the President and the savants. The sounds of gunfire were so loud and steady one could barely think straight.

James crawled over to Etta and tried to comfort her. Tears ran from her eyes, but she was quiet, twisting her hands together and trying not to lose control. He put his arm around her shoulders and reassured her.

Harvey looked up from the workshop floor, sawdust stuck to his face, his hair a mess. "Is it okay if I cuss now?"

James gave Etta a kiss on her forehead, then inched over to Jeremy. "Hey…Jeremy, I know you know exact world time and all, but would you, by any chance, also know coordinates? Like GPS coordinates?"

Jeremy grinned widely. "Time and coordinates go to…together *oui? Oui*, coordinates. Why do you ask, *mon ami*?

James peered above an overturned work table, and spied the approaching enemy through what used to be the side of the barn. Glancing back at Jeremy, he said, "Be thinking about some coordinates for those tanks out there. I counted six of them. If I can get the laser back online…"

Jeremy smiled broadly and nodded. Then he, too, peeked over the edge of the table. His lips moved quietly as he made calculations in his head.

Suddenly, James stood and walked calmly outside as bullets ripped around him. Approaching the laser, he assessed it for damage and found there was none, it had just lost power. He flipped some switches and turned several knobs, until the tip of the giant laser began to glow red again.

Finney ran out to him and pushed him behind the machine. "Are you crazy, man? You're going to get killed."

James shook his head. "Actually, I've been counting the bullets fired from various weapons and analyzing their trajectory. The odds were, statistically, in my favor."

Finney rolled his eyes in an "I give up" gesture, then rose on one knee and returned fire.

James pulled out his cell phone and called Dr. Edwards. "Are you still in the project operations room, doctor?" he asked.

"Yes, of course. What's happening there?"

"Nothing good. Are you showing our laser back online, by any chance?"

Edwards looked at his computer monitor. "Yes, I'm seeing the laser powered back up. It doesn't show the same power levels, though."

"And the Starfire, is it still in its reversed position, pointing at Earth?"

"Yes…why?"

"Good. I have another target for you, but this one you're going to have to focus a little tighter on or you'll fry the President of the United States. Okay?"

"Excuse me," said Edwards. "I'm not sure I heard that right. It sounded like you said 'fry the President…'"

"Yes, that's correct," said James, "so make it really precise, Dr. Edwards." Then, "Jeremy, how about those coordinates?"

"Okay, try: 81.23 north, 45.66 west. Zee tanks are all nearly in a row, right now. If you fire every 2.5 degrees, moving east to west, you should get zem all."

"You hear that, Dr. Edwards?"

"Yes, James. We're moving Starfire into position. Gonna take a few minutes…"

"We don't have that much time, sir."

Dr. Edwards watched the viewing screen as the huge barrel of the Starfire laser turned, like a giant leviathan changing direction in the sea. It slowed as it came closer to the coordinates they had adjusted it to. "We're almost there, James."

"Lock and load, doc."

Dr. Edwards licked his lips nervously. It was one thing firing this high-powered laser into the sea to save the nation, but to aim it at people was a tougher decision for him. "Are you sure?" he asked.

Finney grabbed James's phone and yelled into it. "This is Homeland Security Director Finney, Dr. Edwards. The President is under attack. Go ahead and fire that damn thing! Now!"

"Yes, sir!" said Edwards, and pushed the button.

Tentacles of red lasers pierced the clouds overhead and found their targets. The tanks glowed red for a moment; the top hatches popped open as men scrambled to escape the heat. Some barely made it as the tanks turned from red to white, glowing with energized heat, then exploded, leaving piles of smoldering metal. Those who were on foot stopped and watched the tanks turn to molten puddles. As a unit, the makeshift soldiers halted their advance and looked around, as if trying to find an explanation for the sudden, unexpected retaliatory attack. Their rank formation began to loosen, then fell apart, as many turned and ran back into the cover of the surrounding forest.

A few of the makeshift militia fired random shots from behind trees, but without a strong leader to guide them, their efforts were half-hearted at best. When a half dozen F-15 fighter jets flew overhead, strafing the ground as they made a pass, the last few holdouts dropped their weapons and raised their hands in surrender.

Finney looked over to James, sweat pouring from his face, panting. "Hey kid, why haven't we been using that laser thing before now?"

James shrugged. "We were, just not for war."

Finney turned to Cooper who emerged from what was left of the workshop. "Mr. President, are you okay?"

"I'm good, Alan. How are you holding up?"

Finney looked at his bloodied shoulder. "Never better, sir. But, I might ask for the weekend off."

Cooper chuckled, then turned and looked around at what was left of the workshop. He did a quick head count of his Secret Service agents, all of whom were still standing. "Thank you, men, for keeping us safe. You did an exemplary job."

He looked sullen for a moment as he stared into the field where the attackers had fled. "I'd still like to have a shot at one of those traitors," he said. Then, he had another thought. "Maybe we still can. Director Finney, would you have the FBI get over to the Portland Trauma Center in Maine? There is a mercenary seaman there who might want to share a story with them. Then have them arrest Vice President Proger for high treason." He ambled over to Finney and put his hand on his shoulder. He pulled back the director's jacket, and sized-up the wound. "You can delegate that order if you'd like. We need to get you to a hospital."

"With all due respect, sir," said Finney. "I'll get the shoulder looked at, but I want to be the one who calls in the arrest for that no good son of a…"

"Eh, no cussing, Mr. Finney," said Harvey. "We're trying to clean up our act around here."

At that, everyone had a much needed laugh.

Cooper approached James and offered his hand. James took it, and shook vigorously. "How am I ever going to express my gratitude—the nation's gratitude—to you and your friends?"

James turned down the corners of his mouth and shrugged. "It's been fun, sir. Really."

"Well," said Harvey. "You could buy me a Dr. Pepper. I'm quite thirsty."

They all had another laugh, though it looked painful for Finney to do so.

CHAPTER THIRTY-ONE

Within a half hour after the last bullet was fired, the Beehive compound was swarming with camera crews, again, along with dozens of police cars, fire engines, and rescue trucks. Finney got into one of them, and was transported to the nearby hospital. He remained on the phone with his key advisors and quickly learned the militia had primarily gathered in the Pennsylvania woods encampment, and their official-unofficial headquarters was the old, closed Brunswick Naval Air Station in southern Maine. He talked to the Defense Director, and had a group of Special Ops soldiers, led by Navy Seal teams, invade and capture those still gathered in those locations.

Finney was also delighted to learn that one of the seamen shot in the assassination attempt in the bar in Maine a few days earlier was in the same hospital as Finney. He paid him a personal visit, and persuaded him to share details about the mission wherein they had found the lost nuclear bomb and moved it to the fault line off Cape Hatteras. He would be the key witness against General Haufman and Vice President Proger when they were tried for treason a few months later.

School buses were commandeered, and the closest U.S. Army personnel carriers were used to round up and transport the captured militia soldiers who had not made it into the cover of the woods. Finney ordered them to be escorted back to their headquarters, which would serve as a makeshift prison to house the marauding militia members. It took over a week, but most of them were captured and detained, either at the base in Brunswick or in county jails as they tried to return to their homes. Most, with the exception of the officers in charge, were eventually given amnesty by President Cooper, who later referred to them as "misguided, misled, and mistaken Americans." As a special token, he treated them all to an IRS audit.

At the Beehive that day, President Cooper—along with James, Etta, Harvey, and Jeremy—returned to the house to check on Dr. Pevnick and his son. Douglas had been the first person to perceive that nature—or some cosmic being that rules the universe—had provided the special message about how to save the country, and Cooper was looking forward to thanking him, personally. But, as they entered the room, they found Dr. Pevnick still kneeling, holding his son's now lifeless hand. Douglas, who had always appeared on the verge of a seizure, or locked in an agonizing grip by his pain, now appeared relaxed, a slight smile on his closed lips, his wracked body at ease.

"He came to," said Pevnick, "just for a moment, and indicated he wanted to write something. You know, his hand started making that motion like before. When he finished…he seemed so at peace. Then, he closed his eyes and just…slipped away." He handed a small sheet of paper to James. "I think this was meant for you."

James scanned the boy's note and smiled. "No, professor. It was actually for you. You see this symbol, here? That means *father*. And this one means *son*."

Pevnick's eyes welled up. "And, what about the other one, the third one, there?"

"Hmm," said James thoughtfully. "That one is a little different. I haven't written it in my Manti language, but it shares elements with other words I've written, or should I say *discovered*, in light of what we've learned recently. I think it means *eternity*."

Pevnick smiled weakly, the skin around his eyes rubbed red, energy drained from him like blood. Exhausted, he laid his head on the edge of his son's bed, and his breathing slowed.

Cooper placed his hands on Pevnick's shoulders and kneaded them for a moment, their close friendship obvious and heartfelt. Then, the group left Pevnick alone to have some final time with his son, and found their way to the kitchen where Mrs. Brown was, once again making tea and cookies.

Mrs. Brown held up a warm tray to the group and within minutes its contents were reduced to crumbs. Even tiny Etta gorged ravenously on the cookies.

The room's small television flashed a news report showing Vice President Proger being led out of his office in Washington, flanked by Secret Service agents in dark suits, their faces expressionless. Proger stopped to address the surrounding media.

Mrs. Brown said, "Oh, I'm sorry, Mr. President. You probably don't want to watch this." She reached for the knob to turn it off.

"Are you kidding?" said Cooper. "Leave it on, please. I think I'm going to enjoy this."

"This is a miscarriage of justice," Proger snarled into the cameras. "America needed a strong leader and I was only trying to fill that role."

One of the reporters pushed ahead and managed to get his question in. "How do you respond to the accusation that the reason America needed a strong leader was because you tried and failed to use a nuclear bomb that could have killed millions of people to levy a political coup?"

Cooper smiled, and said, "I like that guy."

"It's all conjecture..." Proger tried to go on, but one of the agents grabbed him by the back of a neck, like a prison guard pushing a prisoner back into his cell, and stuffed the Vice President into a waiting car, his hair mussed, his face indignant, as the agent said, "Oh, shut up."

Cooper laughed. "I like him, too."

The U.S. Attorney General, Richard Murphy, a handsome, polished-looking young man with a face that held promise, interrupted the crowd of reporters. "As your Attorney General, the President has tasked me with the investigation of this case of treason. We have substantial evidence showing the Vice President's duplicity and involvement in this unprecedented act of domestic terrorism..."

Later that night, an exhausted Dr. Pevnick, and the savants, finished an incredible dinner that Mrs. Brown prepared for them. Pevnick glanced around at his unusual guests as they counted their clothes and bites of food; as Jeremy bent his fork into some sort of sculpture that mimicked a Brancusi; as Harvey read several books in between courses; as Etta and James slipped over to a piano in a dimly-lit corner of the room. They sat close together as James played Pachelbel's Canon in D Major for her, and she laid her head on his shoulder. The scene and the music were so beautiful Pevnick had to leave the room, so no one could see him cry.

***

Two Days Later.

President Cooper held a press conference to answer post-crisis questions and acknowledge the help he received in mitigating the disaster. He was humble but strong, accompanied, once again, by Dr. Pevnick and the savants.

"Throughout American history," he said, addressing the country, "there have been incidents of high treason, and while we like to think of ourselves as a civilized nation—indeed, a brotherhood—we are constantly reminded that we do not always hold the same ideologies. Those of us who hold the Constitution as the founding document of law must always be ready to defend it. We must always be on guard against not only foreign threats, but also those enemies who come from within, who would challenge our system of justice, our way of life. And we must, at times, look to the outside of what we ordinarily believe to be the only way to solve problems, to find new ways to move forward, ways none of us could possible conceive."

He paused and looked up at the crowd, then back to Pevnick and the savants. "A couple of days ago, when I met with the press, I could not fully reveal to you, the citizens of this great nation, the extent or even the intent, of the crisis we were facing. It was on a scale beyond any of our notions, whether scientifically or politically, and beyond the scope of our knowledge in disaster preparedness. But, we all learned some hard lessons, especially myself. The lesson I learned was never to judge a book by its cover. Someone I thought was a friend and an advisor turned out to be a traitor of an unprecedented category in history. And a group of people I did not know nor admittedly, particularly believe in, gave me insight into not only what man can still do, but what *faith* can still do, if we hold onto it.

"Over the next few weeks and months, we will be offering economic aid to those persons who suffered from this act of domestic terrorism. We will be reinforcing our stateside troops and National Guard to protect us from future incidents, if they should occur, and we will, once again, increase our aid to the scientific community and the many wonderful possibilities it holds. For now, I want to thank this small group of people, these heroes."

Cooper turned to the savants and held out his hand as each came up to be greeted and introduced. "Mr. James Tramwell, from England, one of our greatest allies; Mr. Harvey Peet, from Australia; Ms. Etta Kim, from Japan; Mr. Jeremy Clemens, from France; and last, but certainly not least, a true professional and close personal friend, Dr. Stephen Pevnick. Dr. Pevnick's son, Douglas, may he rest in peace, was instrumental in helping mitigate this crisis and, quite possibly, opened up a whole new world of communication and understanding for those among us who may speak in a language beyond simple words. Thank you all for not only saving this great nation, but for restoring in me, and in those few lucky to know you, our faith in God and our belief in the impossible. Ladies and gentlemen, please give a warm reception to these extraordinary people."

The crowd, a great many of them seasoned press people eager for a story, took a momentary pause from that commitment, and gave a generous offering of accolades. Amidst the noise of celebration, one reporter was able to get to a microphone and belt out a question.

"This is a remarkable story, Mr. President. I'm sure we owe all of you a great debt. But, the world goes on, and disasters are occurring more and more often. We learned less than an hour ago, for instance, that a significant earthquake occurred in the Canary Islands. It's believed it's only a matter of days, if not hours, until a giant tsunami is produced in the sea off northwestern Africa that will threaten hundreds of thousands of lives. Will America be able to respond to another crisis and, if so, what can we possibly do to mitigate these disasters?"

Cooper began to respond to the young reporter's question. He had been anticipating it, having heard about the impending crisis, but the truth was, he really had no answer.

James and the group had been standing off to one side after their introductions, meeting and greeting various members of the press and elected officials. But with the mention of future disasters, his ears perked up, and he stepped up to the microphone beside President Cooper.

"Do you mind, Mr. President?" he asked.

Cooper, surprised but trusting him, said, "Why...no, James."

"I...uh," began James, slowly at first, then gaining confidence, "I...sort of...anticipated the problem in the Canary Islands, and... well...I have an idea...."

THE END

ACKNOWLEDGMENTS

Thank you to all my beta readers: My wife, Lisa, always the first to read through my coffee-stained pages. Louis Lara, Kayla Van Mehren, Varsha Chandra, Sarah Salmela, Lisa MacMillan, Vanessa Van Sycle; thank you all for contributing your time and thoughts. To my editors: Dawn Scovill, Amy Lignor, and especially John and Shannon Raab—you are doing wonderful things for so many writers. Shannon, your art is unparalleled.

ABOUT THE AUTHOR

Patrick Kendrick is an award winning author of several thrillers, including: *Papa's Problem*, a Florida Book Award and Hollywood Film Festival Award winner. *Extended Family*, which earned a starred review from Booklist. His newest crime thriller, *Acoustic Shadows*, was published by HarperCollins in June and is a Royal Palm Literary Award Finalist. *The Savants*, a sci-fi, political thriller is his first YA novel, and is published by Suspense Publishing. A former firefighter and freelance journalist, he lives in Florida close to the sea.

Facebook: https://www.facebook.com/patrick.
kendrick.142
Twitter: @authorkendrick
Web site: www.talesofpatrickkendrick.com

Made in the USA
Lexington, KY
17 October 2016